Eight Keys

Eight Keys

SUZANNE LaFLEUR

SCHOLASTIC INC.

ISBN 978-0-545-48797-9

Text copyright © 2011 by Suzanne M. LaFleur.
All rights reserved. Published by Scholastic Inc., 557 Broadway, New York, NY 10012,
by arrangement with Wendy Lamb Books, an imprint of Random House Children's Books,
a division of Random House, Inc. SCHOLASTIC and associated logos are trademarks
and/or registered trademarks of Scholastic Inc.

12 11 10 9 8 7 6 5 4 3 2 1   12 13 14 15 16 17/0

Printed in the U.S.A.   40

First Scholastic printing, September 2012

The text of this book is set in Goudy.
Book design by Stephanie Moss

For Erika,
who has shared several keys with me

Part I

Why My Life Really Stinks

The trouble all started right before the first day of sixth grade, the last time Franklin and I played Knights.

Knights works like this: we get our swords, we head out to the woods, and we go on chivalrous missions to battle ghost knights.

Uncle Hugh made our wooden swords when we were six, which is when we came up with the game. Franklin's mom wasn't happy about him making us weapons, but Uncle Hugh assured her that the worst that could happen was we would get splinters—and that's only happened a couple times.

We never really battle each other.

Or at least, we never had before.

Franklin met me in the woods with his purple bicycle helmet on. Some days he wears his helmet when we play. It's weird, but I don't say anything about it. It's not like it matters, anyway.

Franklin almost always begins the game. He did that day, too.

"Kneel before me," he announced in his deepest voice.

I knelt and bowed my head. "Your quest shall be to find the missing cast of King Alberto."

"I think it's a cask," I interrupted in a regular voice, looking up. "With a *k*."

"I'm not sure," Franklin admitted, also in his regular voice. Then he whispered, as if it were a secret from the game, "What is that, anyway?"

"I don't know."

Franklin shrugged, put his serious face back on, and continued in his deep voice. "You are to find the missing cask-t of King Alberto. Rise, Sir Knight, and go forth upon your quest."

He tapped my shoulders lightly with his sword. I stood and knocked his sword with mine, which was his signal to go forth upon the same quest.

We took off, slowly at first, until Franklin yelled, "Ghost knight, behind you!" I stopped to battle the phantom who aimed to ruin our quest. Franklin let out another scream and ran past me to battle a few more ghosts.

My ghost killed by decapitation, I paused for a minute to watch Franklin. He looked funny, swinging his sword and yelling at things that weren't really there. I had never thought about what we looked like playing. Was it a silly thing to do, really?

An abandoned cardboard box lay close by.

I summoned my deepest voice.

"Halt, human!" I yelled. "Halt!"

Franklin stopped, breathing hard. "Yes . . . Good Knight?"

"Good Lady," I corrected in my deep voice.

"Huh?" he asked, in his regular voice.

"I am a lady knight," I said.

"There are no lady knights," he said.

"Of course there are. I am a lady ghost knight, possessing the body of the knight you thought you knew. And I have found your sacred casket, and it belongs to me." I set my foot on the cardboard box like an explorer stepping off his ship onto new land. "You have no choice but to fight me."

Franklin thought for only a second before falling back into the game.

"You shall never have our sacred casket, demon! And I shall free my fellow knight from your possession!"

He dove at me, sword outstretched, and I met his sword with my own. There was no neat clash of metal, just a dull *thunk* of wood smacking wood. We both hit hard. After a few strong hits, which sent Franklin darting backward, I turned and ran, scooping up the cardboard box—the cast or cask or casket or whatever-it-was now—looking back to swipe at Franklin every few feet. He was putting up a good fight. This was definitely one of the best games of Knights we had ever played.

But when you're playing Knights in the woods, you have to be careful of these things all at once: where you swing your sword, that you don't drop your treasure, and that you look where you're going.

It's not hard to guess which one I forgot.

We came to a stretch of the woods where the path ran above a steep hill. I twisted to take another hit at Franklin, but my front foot slipped, and I fell.

After the world had stopped tumbling, I heard "Elise, Elise, Elise, Elise!"—Franklin hurrying after me through all the rocks and leaves and vines and shrubs and prickers that lined the hill.

"Next time," Franklin panted, when he'd caught up with me where I was lying curled up in a ball, "you should wear kneepads. Kneepads and shin guards."

The front of my legs, from my knees to my ankles, ended up covered in bloody streaks. Aunt Bessie made me sit for her to clean all the cuts, but they dried in yucky scabs all over me for my first day at my new middle school. Aunt Bessie and Uncle Hugh both vetoed the long jeans I was wearing to hide my wounds.

"It's too darn hot for that sort of silliness! You'll pass out!" declared Uncle Hugh.

"The material will rub against those cuts and open them right up," insisted Aunt Bessie.

I sat on the edge of the bathtub in my shorts with a box of Band-Aids—plain ones, thank goodness—and stuck them all over my legs. When I had a crisscross of at least twenty peach bandages over my tan legs, I realized that trying to hide the scabs was even worse that just letting them show. I rested my head on my knees and then let out a huge "Grrr!" of frustration.

"Elise! The bus will be coming." Aunt Bessie peeked around the door. "Do you want us to walk you?"

"No," I said. As I walked out the front door, some of the Band-Aids drooped off my legs, not sticking on one side. I grabbed one to yank it off, but the other side was tightly glued to the hairs on my leg. "Ow!" I yelled as it ripped off. I added "Bye!" before leaving Uncle Hugh and Aunt Bessie standing on the porch, looking kind of worried.

When I made it to the bus stop, the usual kids from our grade were there: Franklin plus Sam, Ben, Stewart, and Diana. I had never really gotten to know the other boys, and what I knew about Diana was that she wore funny cat sweaters. Because it was hot, she was in a cat T-shirt. Pink, with a black-and-white cat patched on in other materials.

"Hi," she said.

"Hi," I answered.

"I went to camp all summer and there was no electricity and no real toilets."

"Sounds awesome," I said, not sure if that was awesome. Talking with Diana always made me feel uncomfortable. She was so weird.

The older kids who had gone off to middle school before us were clumped together a few yards away, talking and laughing and ignoring us. No parents had come to the bus stop.

Once we got on the bus, it was totally like usual—just me and Franklin on our own, in our own seat, having our own conversation. That was how the whole school day always used to go. We didn't really need to get to know the other kids because we had each other.

Franklin, of course, didn't comment on my yucky legs. It was like he couldn't see them, even though I couldn't help but stare at them the whole time, thinking about how messed up they looked. He was suddenly Mr. School Facts, telling me all these things about what can go wrong at middle school. You could be placed in the wrong math class, be picked on by eighth graders, fail to conjugate verbs properly in language class (whatever that means). . . . Then he moved on to all these worries about *our* middle school, which has three different elementary schools feeding into it. There would be hundreds of kids there we didn't know. And then he actually calculated how many that would be by taking the average number of kids per grade in our area's elementary schools and multiplying that by the number of grades in the middle school and multiplying *that* by the number of feeder schools (minus ours, of course) and by the time he had gotten to the answer I was definitely Not Listening.

It didn't matter how many new kids there were at school. It took only one to ruin my life.

When I sat down in homeroom, my backpack scraped against my legs.

"Crap," I muttered, running my hand over my skin, getting blood on my fingers. I hoped no one had noticed and quickly wiped my hand on my shorts. The girl next to me made a disgusted face, rolled her eyes, and shifted away from me.

The teacher handed out sheets of paper with locker assignments. There are so many middle schoolers at our school that sixth graders have to have partners—which is, apparently, totally okay according to the teachers, because sixth graders' textbooks aren't as thick as seventh and eighth graders' books. So while I can look forward to one day having my own locker, I also get to look forward to having really humongous books and backaches from carrying them around.

The locker assignments seemed to be alphabetical, because across from my name, Elise Bertrand, was Amanda Betterman.

We were given twenty minutes to set up our lockers. In the hall, I followed the numbers until I found 2716, and who should show up at the same time but the girl who'd sat next to me in homeroom. I recognized her long, streaky brown hair, held off her forehead by two clips, and her tiny white skirt.

"Oh, gag. I have to share with the Bloody Queen of Scabs." Several kids standing around her looked at my legs and laughed. Then Amanda said to me, very seriously, "Please don't get blood on my things. I don't want to get any weird diseases."

"I don't have any weird diseases."

To make everything one hundred times better (not), who should show up but Sir Franklin, needing to stick up for me. "It's no big deal, she just got hurt playing Knights."

Which was not the right thing to say. At all.

"What's Knights?"

"It's a pretend game."

Amanda smirked. "Playing pretend. That sounds *really cool.*"

But the way she said it meant the opposite: *so not cool.*

The other kids started laughing at me and Franklin. Kids we didn't know but also a couple kids we'd known since kindergarten.

Apparently *cool* sixth graders don't play. They definitely don't play Knights. They have streaky hair and short skirts.

But there I was on the first day of school with scabby knees like a kindergartener, and my best friend got me pegged as a baby.

One Last Visit to Summer

The first day of school is always a Thursday or Friday. I like it because we get a little snatch of summer back over the weekend. This year's Friday start meant I woke up on Saturday completely relieved to have two days off from school. I was in no hurry to go back there.

And it *was* like having summer back. I lay in bed until my door creaked open.

"Hi, Franklin," I said.

The clock said it was nine, but it was still very dark in my room. Having a first-floor bedroom with the porch outside means that sunshine never bothers me in the morning.

"Hi." Franklin came in and sat on my bed. "What do you want to do today?"

I thought for a minute, and Franklin let me think. He would never interrupt when I am thinking.

"I want to figure out the best things we did all summer, and then do them again."

"Okay. Here, I'll make a list." He got a yellow notepad and pencil from my desk and sat back down on my bed. "I really liked the day we found frogs at the stream. We could do that again."

"Okay."

"Knights?"

"No Knights."

"Why not?"

"I'm not better from the last time we played Knights," I said, feeling the smooth sheets against my rough, scabby legs. And I wasn't better from getting made fun of. This was the weekend; I wanted to push school way out of my mind, to forget that yesterday had ever happened.

"What else, then?" He tapped the pencil's eraser on the paper.

"I liked helping Uncle Hugh finish the furniture." Uncle Hugh is a craftsman. He makes things out of wood, like rocking chairs and tables and cabinets.

Franklin added it to the list.

"And I liked when Aunt Bessie let us make ice cream."

"Lactose-free?" Franklin asked.

"Of course," I said. A glimmer of excitement lit Franklin's eyes. His mom limits his sugar at home, but we always have plenty for him at my house. Franklin can't have any real dairy products because of his allergies, but Aunt Bessie's pretty much a genius about getting around that. She really can make anything. She does catering out of our house, so we have a special up-to-code kitchen with stainless steel countertops and lots of fancy appliances.

"I liked looking at the slides on my microscope." Franklin

finished writing everything. "That's probably enough for today . . . what do you want to do first?"

"Let me see if we can do the stuff with Uncle Hugh and Aunt Bessie today at all." Aunt Bessie and I cook together on Saturdays if she doesn't have a catering job, but if she did she'd be busy all day.

I climbed out of bed and decided that the tank top I'd slept in would do for the day, too, so I found my shorts on the floor and pulled them on. I didn't mind getting dressed with Franklin around, especially since he was always certain to fix his eyes on a point on the wall and stare straight ahead. Which is sort of silly, because I know he still wears cartoon underwear. How can you be embarrassed around someone who knows about your cartoon underwear?

I picked a T-shirt up off the floor and threw it at Franklin's head to signal him that I was done and it was safe to move his eyes around the room again.

"All ready?" he asked.

"Yup." I slid into some flip-flops as I headed to find Aunt Bessie.

Aunt Bessie was in her chef's clothes, which are black even though chef's clothes are usually white. She and I agree that black looks nicer, cleaner, and more slimming for her plump figure than white. She used to be a redhead; now that she's in her fifties, her hair is dull orange and pepper gray, but she still wears it pulled back in the same long, thick braid. She was carrying trays to load into her catering van.

"When will you be back?" I asked.

"This afternoon."

"Can we make end-of-the-summer ice cream?"

"I'll set aside some fresh strawberries for it. Does that sound good?"

"Yum! I mean, yes!"

Aunt Bessie went to set the trays on the racks in the van. That's a job that Franklin and I are *not* allowed to help with. She doesn't consider us strong or steady enough. It would never be worth the time it might save in the event that a tray was dropped.

"Ice cream later," I promised Franklin when he followed me out onto the porch. His eyes got all big and shiny and sugar-hungry again. "Now for Uncle Hugh."

We headed across the large gravel circle of the driveway in front of our house to the barn.

The barn isn't old and falling-down like a lot of barns. It was renovated, complete with electricity and a bathroom and an open elevator to the second floor, so that Uncle Hugh could have his workshop there. On the second floor is a hall-way lined with shut doors only about as far apart as horse stalls would be, except for the two on either end, which are a little farther away. Once when I was little, I climbed up the stairs (I was never, ever allowed to play in the elevator) and counted the doors: eight. I was trying all the doorknobs when I heard Aunt Bessie behind me.

"They're all locked, Elise," she said, holding her hand out to me. I took it. "Let's stay downstairs." We walked back down to Uncle Hugh's workshop. What she meant was I wasn't to go up to try to open the doors, and I wasn't to play upstairs in the barn, and I wasn't to worry about what was up there. It was probably dangerous equipment for Uncle Hugh's work.

"Hey, Cricket," Uncle Hugh greeted me as Franklin and I came into the barn. He's been calling me Cricket since I learned to talk in full sentences and wouldn't shut up. I don't talk all the time like that anymore, but he says all those interesting things I'm not saying are still whirring around in my head.

"Is there anything to finish?"

"Nope. Actually, I just finished finishing." Uncle Hugh chuckled to himself, rubbing his hands over the legs of a table. "I have to go out on deliveries."

"So there's nothing we can help with?"

"Not at the moment. But you're welcome to play with the scrap pieces."

Uncle Hugh puts any extra small pieces in a bin for me and Franklin to build with and leaves out some nails and two hammers. We've made plenty of neat things. I looked at Franklin, who was still holding the torn-off piece of yellow paper and the pencil. He shook his head at me. "Not on the list."

"List—?" Uncle Hugh started, but then he changed his mind. Whenever he asks about what Franklin and I are up to, he gets a really long explanation that he'd rather not hear. "Well, I'm heading out. You can play with that stuff if you want. You know never to touch anything else in here. Just don't tell your mother, Franklin, she wouldn't like you in here on your own."

"Aye-aye," Franklin answered, with a salute. Then he turned to me. "Frogs next, I think."

Franklin and I ran out of the barn and across the fields next to my house until they became a few sparse trees, until they became the woods, until we reached the stream.

When we got there, we stood still, trying to slow our breathing, because it was hard to hear the frogs. Frogs don't say "ribbit" or "croak" like everyone thinks they do. They sound like rubber bands. A whole concert of plucked rubber bands: *bung, bung!* After a minute of listening hard and hearing only the gentle movement of the stream, I said, "There are no frogs here."

"There have to be some," Franklin said. "It's still warm out." He put the paper and pencil in his back pocket and sat down to pull off his shoes. Franklin's mom insists on sneakers and socks every day. She doesn't know that most days, at some point, Franklin leaves his shoes behind. Early in the summer I pulled a splinter out of his foot with tweezers because he didn't want to have to tell her about it.

Franklin stepped gently into the ankle-deep water and started looking along the moist rocks.

"See anything?" I asked.

"No."

"I told you, there are no frogs here. They're all gone."

Franklin searched with his eyes. Then he sighed, giving up.

"Slides?" I asked.

"Oh!" Franklin took a small tube out of his pocket, uncapped it, and dipped it into the stream. "I want a sample of the water. We can look and see if there are any organisms in it."

"Good idea," I said. I didn't care quite as much about that stuff as Franklin, but I did have fun playing scientist with him all summer, pretending that we would discover something big.

Franklin squished his wet feet back into his socks and shoes and we walked to his house. He's one of my closest neighbors, but still, he lives pretty far away. You can't see any other houses from mine.

Franklin's big farmhouse is a lot like ours, but it feels nothing like it on the inside. At our house there's hustle and bustle and very few rules—at his there are plenty of rules and almost nothing going on.

As soon as we got inside, his mother, tall and thin, swooped upon us.

"Good morning, Elise. I assume you had a good breakfast?"

"Good morning, Mrs. White," I answered. "I—uh—forgot about breakfast."

Franklin's face went expressionless. We both knew what was about to happen.

"Well, come, come to the kitchen," Mrs. White said. "We must have breakfast. I will make you eggs and toast. Franklin ate breakfast before he went over to fetch you."

Franklin gave me a smug look. We sat down at the kitchen table and he opened *Scientific American* and started reading. I waited for my fate, which was soon delivered in the form of over-easy eggs and unbuttered wheat toast. I said thank you and started eating. Mrs. White's eggs seemed slimy compared to Aunt Bessie's. Even Uncle Hugh's are better. Even *my own* attempts at frying eggs are better.

Franklin's mother sat down with us and watched me eat as if it made her really happy.

"There now. You know how important a good start is. Doesn't anyone make sure you get breakfast?"

Of course Aunt Bessie and Uncle Hugh make sure I eat, but I'm not a baby. They know I can make my own breakfast. Franklin has probably never made any food for himself.

"They were both working this morning," I said. "I'm in charge of my own breakfast."

I could tell Mrs. White didn't think eleven-year-olds in charge of breakfast was a good idea.

If that's what natural parents are like, who needs them? I'd take Uncle Hugh and Aunt Bessie any day.

I don't really think about Mom or Dad much. They are mostly just an empty space inside me, a forgotten feeling from long ago. I never knew Mom at all, because she died when I was born, and Dad was gone when I was three. After the doctor told Dad he had a year or two to live, he wrote me a bunch of letters for my birthdays, so I hear from him once a year. Uncle Hugh has the letters—somewhere, I don't know where, I've looked.

I decided, as I finished the last runny bite of egg and abandoned the toast crust, that I would have to be more careful about truthful answers. It wouldn't be such a harmful lie to say I'd already eaten, would it?

Mrs. White cleared my empty plate. "What are you up to?"

Franklin looked up from his magazine. "We're going to look at my slides. I collected a new sample."

"That sounds fun. Be careful with the glass pieces, though."

"We will," I promised. "C'mon."

Franklin and I went up to his room, where he cleared a bunch of other science projects off his desk and set up his microscope. He took out a slide and set it flat on his desk. He found the little tube in his pocket and carefully took off the top. He strapped on some safety goggles, closed one eye and concentrated with the other as he slowly dripped a couple drops of stream water onto the glass. Still working with one eye, he got another tiny glass plate and lowered it onto the first.

"Ah! Help me!" I shrieked in a tiny, high-pitched voice.

Franklin looked at me with his one open eye.

"Those are the organisms," I explained. "Screaming because they are squished."

"You should be wearing goggles," Franklin said. "What if the glass breaks?"

I got the other pair of safety goggles, the purple-tinted ones, and strapped them on. Wearing them makes the experiment feel more serious, but, at the same time, the fact that they are sized for an eight-year-old also makes the whole thing seem more silly. I felt like a bug, or like my eyes were squished organisms.

Once the slide was secured under the clasps on the microscope, Franklin permitted our goggles to come off so that we could peer through the lens.

"I see all kinds of cool things!" Franklin looked and looked, and I let him look, the way he lets me think.

"I'm going to get to work on my sketch," he announced

finally, finding some graph paper on his bookshelf and setting his colored pencils out in front of him on the desk. It was my turn.

I could make out green flecks speckling the clear water, but not whether they were moving or breathing or living at all. I don't think I could see what Franklin saw. I looked for a long time anyway, pretending.

I glanced at Franklin's drawing so far. It had lots of little oblong shapes and ovals.

I started my own drawing, but it was really a copy of Franklin's. Every few minutes he looked through the lens again to get details right, which was when I would study his graph paper. Being a proper pretend scientist, I also got up to check the microscope every few minutes.

"What do you think these little green blobbies do?" I asked.

"Probably they cure cancer," Franklin said.

"Really, you think?"

"Sure. We can bottle stream water and sell it."

"If the cure for cancer was just drinking stream water, why wouldn't everyone already be doing it?"

"Well, you see the little purply specks?" Franklin asked.

"Uh-huh." Both of our drawings now had tiny purple dots.

"Those are a terrible bacteria. They eat your innards from the inside out," Franklin said. "They'd probably kill you faster than the cancer would."

"Oh no!" I acted stunned. "Well, it's obvious what we need to do!"

"I know!" Franklin said. "Separate the green blobbies out from the purple specks."

"But how?"

"Spinning them really fast."

I picked up the tube where the leftover stream water was and started spinning around really fast. Franklin unlatched the slide and started spinning around, too. Soon we were dizzy and laughing. When Franklin started to slow down to catch his breath, I yelled, "No! Don't stop! Spin faster!"

We were interrupted by a knock on the door. Three hours had passed, and it was lunchtime. Mrs. White had already set plates on the table with ham sandwiches and five celery and five carrot sticks each. Franklin's dad ate lunch with us, but he read the *Wall Street Journal* the whole time.

After lunch, the thrill of science had worn off. We wandered back to my house.

"How does the list look?" I asked Franklin.

"Well . . ." He took the yellow paper out of his pocket. "No helping Uncle Hugh, no frogs, microscope done. Now for ice cream."

Aunt Bessie wasn't home yet, so we waited on the porch. Franklin lay on his back and counted the boards in the ceiling. I noticed my backpack was still there, full of books and homework, but no way was I working on that. No way was that bag being opened. No way was it going inside, either. School would not enter my house yet.

The awful girl at school . . . that was just a first-day thing, right? Maybe she was just being mean because she was nervous about starting school, too. Maybe over the weekend everyone would forget about it.

Aunt Bessie finally drove up with her truck full of empty trays (we *were* allowed to carry those), several plastic containers of leftovers, and two big containers of strawberries. Not big, fake, shiny grocery-store ones, but real ones, small, juicy, and deep red. Aunt Bessie saw me put one in my mouth and she swatted my hand. "Aren't we making ice cream?" But then she ate one, too, and smiled.

We used the electric ice cream maker. The sugar and soy yogurt whirled and whirled, and then it had to sit. For hours. More hours.

Uncle Hugh came home and we all made tacos. Tacos are great, but Franklin and I just wanted the ice cream to be ready.

When it finally, finally was, we took our bowls out onto the porch. I wanted mine to melt, after all that time waiting for it to freeze. I ate slowly, feeling the cold of the spoon as I pulled it back out of my mouth each time. Franklin ate quickly, probably hoping for seconds before he had to go home.

The sun was starting to set.

"The day is totally over," I said. "What did you think?"

Franklin paused his eating to look at me, surprised. "It was fun."

"There was nothing all that special about it," I said. "It was just a regular day. We only did half the things on our list."

"Fifty percent," Franklin said.

"Right, fifty percent." I stirred my ice cream to soften it some more. I noticed my backpack still sitting there, full of work to do: the get-to-know-you survey from the language arts teacher, the chapter to read and the questions to answer on the scientific method, the math review of multiplication and division. . . .

"You know what the best thing about the summer was?" I asked.

"What?"

"Not having a to-do list."

Franklin was quiet for a minute. "We have one more day," he pointed out.

So on Sunday we didn't make a list. We started off with a *Star Wars* movie, and when it was over we just popped in the next one. After our third *Star Wars* movie, Uncle Hugh asked if we wanted pizza, so of course we said yes. When the pizza was delivered he let us bring it right into the den. We each ate the way we like to, me layering two slices one on top of the other, cheese on the inside (a pizza sandwich), Franklin pulling off most of the cheese in one big triangle and then picking off every little bit that might have been left behind. Aunt Bessie always tells him we can get something else, but he says he really likes pizza.

After the pizza and the movies were all done, Aunt Bessie put out ice cream and little dishes of all kinds of toppings on the kitchen counter. The ice cream—sticky-creamy store-bought vanilla (lactose-free, again)—was the perfect base for a sundae of fudge and strawberry sauce and M&M's and sprinkles.

And that day was perfect. It was perfect because there was nothing to go right or wrong, it just *was*.

I didn't think of my backpack again, not even once. Not even when I went with Uncle Hugh to give Franklin a ride home in the dark, not even when we came home, not even when I lay in bed feeling the first cool breeze that came in through my windows, telling me that summer was over.

3

Things Get Worse

Monday totally sucked.

When Franklin and I walked into school together, some boy I didn't even know said, "*Play* anything fun this weekend?"

My cheeks felt hot. Franklin didn't get that this was teasing. He opened his mouth: "Ye—" and I elbowed him lightly to *shut up*.

At my locker, Amanda had a crew with her: three girls in flat shoes, skirts, and fitted shirts. I guess dressing up wasn't a first-day-of-school thing but an all-the-time thing. I could never go to school like that. How uncomfortable. When I looked down the hallway, there were more girls in nice clothes than last week. Because of Amanda?

"How're the scabs, Scabular?"

Too bad I couldn't say something strong: *They're great, how are you?* All I could think about was how I must look like a boy dressed in my jeans and sneakers and red sweatshirt. The weather had gotten cool enough for long clothes; Amanda couldn't even see my scabs. But if she was still talking about them, would it matter if they were hidden or went away? Maybe I'd be known as scab-girl forever.

I'd just been staring at Amanda while the thoughts whirred in my head, not saying anything. I must have looked like an empty-headed ding-dong. She laughed, and a couple of her friends did the same. Then they all walked away.

If you forgot your homework in elementary school, the teacher just said that you could bring it tomorrow.

In middle school, the teachers seemed interested in making examples.

Like the science teacher. Mr. Fleming collected the homework and then noticed that some of us didn't hand anything in.

"Who didn't hand in homework this morning?" he asked.

Three other kids raised their hands. I snuck mine up slowly, afraid to admit it but more afraid to be caught lying.

"Maybe you got away with not doing your homework back in elementary school, but that won't be the case now. You're starting the year with zeros on your assignments. You're not making a good impression. You're not off to a good start."

Franklin watched me slouch in my chair. Hadn't he been with me the whole weekend?

Mr. Fleming turned to write on the board. "When did you do your homework?" I whispered to Franklin.

"Friday afternoon when I got home."

"Talking during the lesson is not okay, either," Mr. Fleming announced, back still turned.

It went pretty much the same way in the other classes.

I felt like a moron for not having any work done. Once

I thought about it, I remembered that there *were* kids in elementary school who got into trouble for not having their homework done. I never knew how those kids ended up not doing it so much. Back then you only had one teacher, so at the most there were two things to do in one night; now we had seven different teachers and they all gave their own assignments!

I was so glad when school was over. We didn't take the bus home. We went to see Leonard instead.

Leonard was my dad's best friend. They grew up together. Dad moved away for college and work for a while, but he moved back here to have his family near his brothers and Leonard. Leonard owns the hardware store in town, and he lets me and Franklin help out and make a little money whenever we want. Leonard's like my extra uncle.

I love the hardware store because everybody who works there knows me. And it has that great smell, like paint and cedar chips; that might be my favorite smell in the world. I walk in and I just feel better.

Franklin went to talk to some of the other guys. He always does that first, to let me say hi to Leonard by myself.

I headed to the back counter. Leonard's easy to spot: tall with thinning hair, bright green Town Center Hardware apron.

"Hey, Cricket. What's new?"

"Nothing."

"How's sixth grade going?"

"Awful."

"Why's that?"

"Yucky new teachers, yucky new kids, yucky more homework . . ."

"Yucky, huh?"

"Yeah, everything is yucky."

"Well, give it a chance. This is only your—what?—second day?"

I nodded.

"Are you and Franklin in need of an ice cream?" Leonard placed several quarters on the counter.

"Should we sweep up? Or inventory the nails? Or stir paint?"

"Nah, no need." Leonard smiled. "Ice cream's on the house today."

"Thanks, Leonard," I said. I slid the quarters off the counter into my other palm.

"Bye, Cricket."

"Bye!" As I left, I called to Franklin, who seemed to be showing a customer what kind of nails would be best for the wood he was planning to use. Franklin knows too many random things.

We went next door to the ice cream place. Franklin always gets a blue raspberry slushie. I picked M&M ice cream. I don't like the way frozen M&M's hurt your teeth, but I love how the colors come off the candies and streak the vanilla ice cream rainbow.

Franklin and I sat at a table with high chairs. I decided not to tease him about his blue mouth, but it was really hard not to. The light stain around his lips made me think of a five-year-old.

Aunt Bessie came to pick us up at four o'clock. I thought about getting right to my homework. But I'd been at school all day. I needed a break.

"What do you want to do?" Franklin asked.

"I don't know." I thumped my backpack down on the porch. "Not homework."

"Let's build stuff," Franklin said. "It looked like Uncle Hugh just put out a whole bunch of pieces for us."

"Yeah, okay." I could make something that *I* wanted to make, not do something that a teacher said I had to do.

Uncle Hugh's truck was gone, so he wasn't in his workshop. Franklin got the bin of wood pieces and dumped them out on an empty table. I got our hammers and nails.

"What do you want to make?" I asked.

"Let's build a castle."

"Don't you think of castles as more rock than wood?"

"We can paint it to look like gray rocks. Or maybe we can build with sugar cubes on the outside and paint those. It'll be great. Here, you make the base and I'll make a tower."

I made a floor and then a four-sided structure. Franklin's tower took a lot longer because he wanted it to have more than four sides. He was being quiet, so I started to wander around the barn.

There are different sections of the barn off the main workshop. Uncle Hugh uses them to store equipment, supplies, and projects in progress. Mostly he's hired to build specific things, but he also makes things just because he feels like it and sells those, too. In one room was a rocking chair that he was staining a beautiful blue, in between light blue and green, the color uneven in a way that made the chair look old and worn. I hoped I could get the chair for my birthday next month. Maybe I could drop the right hints. We don't usually keep any of the things Uncle Hugh makes, because we already have everything we need and they're meant to be sold, after all. Maybe he would make an exception if he knew I really, really wanted it.

The chair looked ready to be sat in—furniture was usually ready to use if he was staining—so I sat in it. I liked the way my arms fit on the armrests, the way my feet just reached the floor, the way the chair tipped gently back and forth.

While I sat there, rocking, something on the wall caught my eye: a key, hanging by string, with a tag. It said *Elise*.

I went over to look closer. I'd never noticed it before, but Uncle Hugh has so much stuff in the barn that it would probably take a lifetime to notice every little thing. How long had the key been there?

I lifted it off the hook.

"Look," I called as I headed back to Franklin. "It has my name on it."

"Huh?" He looked up from connecting the sixth and final side of the tower.

"This key. I've never seen it before. My name's on it. What do you think it goes to?"

"Your room?"

"There's not a lock on my room," I said.

"A treasure chest?"

"A treasure chest? Why would we have a treasure chest?"

"I don't know." Franklin finished nailing the last wall in place. "Come help me attach the tower."

I hung the key back up and went to help.

"I need you to hold the base and the tower together while I nail them, okay?" he asked.

I held them as he counted: "One, two, three."

I watched Franklin hammer. Then suddenly I pictured a tree getting split by lightning. It wasn't just a picture but a hot, splintery feeling in my thumb. I realized I was screaming.

"Oh no, oh no, I'm sorry! Oh no, Elise, come on!"

I was holding my thumb tight with my other hand, so Franklin grabbed my elbow and pulled me out of the barn at a run. In the driveway he started yelling, "Aunt Bessie! Aunt Bessie!"

She came out onto the porch, drying her hands on a towel.

"For heaven's sake," she said. "Oh Lordy, Cricket. Let me see." She examined my hand. It was bleeding now. "How did this happen?"

"We were building, and I hit her," Franklin said.

"With what?"

"A hammer."

"Were nails involved?"

"Yes."

"Car. Now," Aunt Bessie said.

Franklin and I hurried. Franklin asked, "Where are we going?"

"The hospital. Elise, if there's rust in that cut, you'll need a tetanus shot. And if your thumb is actually broken . . . see how it's swelling already? How does it hurt? Dull, sharp?"

"Sharp." I was still crying. Franklin buckled my seat belt. While Aunt Bessie started driving, she had Franklin reach into the emergency kit she keeps in the car and get a disposable ice pack. He slammed it on the cup holder until it turned cold and then held it on my hand.

"I'm sorry, I'm sorry, I'm sorry," he kept saying. I wanted to tell him it was okay, but the words weren't coming out. He's Mr. Super-Careful. What had happened this time?

We waited in the ER for Aunt Bessie to fill out forms and then for the doctors to call us. I had to go by myself for an X-ray. They had me put my arm in a machine. Then the doctor cleaned the cut while we waited for the pictures. I didn't need stitches, but he thought a shot would be a good idea, so he jabbed a needle in my arm. "Clean the cut twice a day and change the bandage."

Aunt Bessie nodded.

"Now let's check out what's going on inside." He put the X-rays up on a board that lit up from behind. He used his pen to point out the bones in my thumb and how there was a crack in one of them. Broken. Not too badly, but broken all the same.

He braced my thumb in a splint, wrapped it in gauze, and put my arm in a soft sling to make sure that I moved my hand as little as possible. I came out looking like I had a fat, bright white thumbs-up strapped to my chest. Awesome.

The doctor had me take pain medicine and handed Aunt

Bessie a slip to get more at the drugstore. Another thing we had to sit around and wait for.

When we dropped Franklin off on the way home, he said, "I'm sorry!" for the one-hundredth time.

"Don't worry," I said. "It's okay."

But maybe it was just the medicine saying that.

Uncle Hugh didn't come home until the baked ziti was ready and cooling on the table. I was sitting there already, my head down, my thumb throbbing.

"Cricket!" he said. "What happened?"

"I went to the hospital."

"I can see that." He sat down next to me. "But why?"

Aunt Bessie made a noise in her throat as she brought the salad to the table. "They were playing in your workshop. Maybe you shouldn't let them play there."

Uncle Hugh turned slightly pink, but he said, "Don't be silly. They know not to touch anything dangerous. Were you using only the things set aside for you?"

"Yes. Just a hammer."

We were quiet while Aunt Bessie served the ziti. Her face was tight, like she had a million things to say.

"Bess," Uncle Hugh said gently. "Accidents can happen anywhere. Playing outside. That happened last week. Walking up and down stairs. Taking a shower. It's good for her and Franklin to have something constructive to do."

"I know." Aunt Bessie softened. "It's just always the

preventable things . . ." The part of the conversation where she might be mad at Uncle Hugh was over.

"How bad is it?" he asked me.

"Broken," I said. "In one place. And cut on the outside. And my fingernail looks pretty ugly."

"What were you building?"

"A castle. Franklin was attaching a tower and I was holding the base."

"Ah. We'll make sure you finish it."

Then we turned to eating for a few minutes, until Aunt Bessie said, "Elise, we have some family news to talk about."

"Family news?" I looked up.

"Yes. I talked to my sister, Annie, today. You remember Annie."

"Of course I do." Annie was years younger than Aunt Bessie, in her thirties; she was nice and fun. She came to our house for dinner a few times a year. "Annie had a baby."

"That's right, she did."

There was a picture of newborn Baby Ava on our family fridge (not Aunt Bessie's work fridge, we don't hang anything on that). Ava looked like an alien, all red with her face smushed.

"Annie and Ava are going to come stay for a while."

"Like for a visit?" I asked. That didn't seem like a reason for the headline "Family News."

Aunt Bessie and Uncle Hugh looked at each other, having one of those private conversations with their eyes.

"To live here for a while."

"What for?" I asked.

"It's nice to be around family when you have a baby. It helps to have support. We have plenty of room here and plenty of us to help."

We do have plenty of room. So much room that my cousins Jake and Alec, Uncle Beau, and Aunt Sally had lived with us for a while when I was little.

"What about the dad?" I sort of remembered a man who'd lived with Annie, but never came here to dinner with her.

"He doesn't live with them."

But . . . "A newborn baby?"

"She's not newborn anymore. Babies grow fast. She's five months old."

"Elise . . . you're spearing your ziti."

I looked at the cold asparagus from the salad that I was poking into my pasta. I looked up at Uncle Hugh, who was laughing silently. "I get it," I said, finally cracking a smile. "Asparagus spear. It's just hard to eat with my left hand, is all."

"We'll give you some more medicine after dinner and get you off to bed," Aunt Bessie promised.

The nighttime version of the medicine made me sleep and sleep until Aunt Bessie woke me up for school in the morning.

Things Get Much Worse

Amanda started laughing the minute I got to our locker. She made a dumb noise and imitated the thumbs-up. "What this time? Playing hospital?"

"You think it's funny that I broke my thumb?" I'm not sure where the guts to say something came from, maybe the medicine Aunt Bessie gave me at breakfast.

Amanda stopped laughing. "Here, let me help you." She opened my backpack, which I had set down on the floor. She took out my paper lunch bag, which had my usual lunch in it: a peanut-butter-and-jelly sandwich and a piece of fruit (which happened to be an orange). She put it in the tall main section of the locker. Then she took my books out of my backpack and dropped them on top of my lunch. I felt sick. Sicker than when the hammer had come crashing down on my thumb.

"There." She gave me a fake sweet smile and handed me my empty backpack. She hung hers on the hook and picked up her books from the floor. "Aren't you going to thank me for helping you?"

I had absolutely nothing to say.

Franklin came up behind me. "Let me carry your things."
I nodded numbly as he collected my books and pencil case.

"That's very sweet," Amanda said. "Retards." Then, thank
God, she left.

It didn't seem to bother Franklin that someone had called
him a retard. "What's her problem?" he asked. But I was
thinking, *What's wrong with us?*

I continued to stand there while Franklin gently set my
lunch on top of the pile in the locker. Even though he was
helping me, I couldn't help but think: *Some of this mess is his
fault.* Or most of it. It was his fault I always looked like a
walking disaster, like a baby, like I couldn't take care of myself
or do things myself.

Some kids in the hall saw my hand and asked what happened. I told them that I broke my thumb, but left out how.
They seemed worried about me. One girl even took markers
and carefully drew a paisley design on the sling. Just as many
kids seemed to have run into Amanda, because they gave me
thumbs-up gestures with goofy noises to go along with them.
I hoped Franklin wouldn't mention that I got hurt *playing*
again. It was making me crazy, listening to him talk about last
night, waiting for him to slip up.

When I got to language arts I remembered I hadn't done
my homework. Again. I decided to talk to the teacher by myself instead of getting in trouble in front of everyone. Things
would have been easier if I'd just had Aunt Bessie write me a
note. But I'd forgotten, so I would have to explain over and
over in each class. While Franklin set our books down on our
desks, I went up to talk to Mrs. Wakefield.

"Elise?" she greeted me, with a question mark, still learning our names.

I nodded.

"What happened?"

"I broke my thumb. I was at the hospital last night and I didn't get to do my homework."

"Well," she said. "Don't worry about it today. Just get it done when you can."

I didn't move from her desk.

"Elise?" Mrs. Wakefield asked. "Are you okay? Are you in pain?"

I didn't know if I should tell her. If she would care. Or if Amanda found out what she would do to me.

"I just—my locker partner—she wrecked my lunch."

"I'm sure it was an accident. It can be hard to share a small space like that."

It *wasn't* an accident, but Mrs. Wakefield said, "Please sit down so I can start class."

I sat. Diana poked me with her pencil.

"Can you help me?" she asked. "I'm doing a class profile for the newspaper."

"A what?"

"An article about the sixth grade. I'm going to interview interesting members of our class."

"You want to interview me?" I asked, feeling a little lighter.

"No," she said. "I thought I'd get your advice about who to interview."

I didn't answer her as Mrs. Wakefield told us to take out our grammar books.

• • •

After school I couldn't even think about playing with Franklin. I hauled my backpack to the table in the family part of the kitchen. Would it be better to do everything for one subject and then move on—knock off being in trouble with teachers one by one? Or do all the homework for tomorrow, and at least that stuff wouldn't be late . . . but it would be hard to answer questions for section three of science before I did the questions for section one . . . and math would be the same story.

I picked to start with Mrs. Wakefield's get-to-know-you survey. Now the problem was having to use my left hand. I had nothing to weigh down the paper and it scootched around when I tried to write. I got so frustrated that I threw my pencil. "Grrr!"

Aunt Bessie came over. "What's the matter?"

"My work looks like it was written by chickens!"

"What does that mean?"

"That's what teachers always say to kids who write messy."

Aunt Bessie smiled, as if she couldn't help it. "You mean chicken scratches."

"It's not funny."

"Here." Aunt Bessie sat down. She slid the paper away from me and found a new pencil. "Your writing hand is injured, and that's difficult. I'll be your scribe."

"You'll write for me?"

"Sure. Whatever you dictate."

I hadn't realized how tight and heavy it had felt inside

my chest until the feeling lifted. I answered Mrs. Wakefield's questions about what my favorite subjects were and who lived in my house with me and what I liked to read, and Aunt Bessie wrote everything down. Then we moved on to math, which was harder, because moving the pencil helps me think. Luckily the beginning-of-the-year review stuff isn't that hard. When Uncle Hugh came in from the barn, expecting dinner, Aunt Bessie hadn't made any and we had gotten through only three assignments. So Uncle Hugh made dinner. He always makes beans and rice. But it was warm and yummy, and afterward I took my social studies book to the den to read.

Aunt Bessie woke me up there later.

"Go to bed, Cricket." She lifted the book from my lap.

"But I only did four assignments."

"How many do you have?"

"Sixteen."

"Sixteen? You can't expect to do them all tonight. You're healing. Tomorrow's another day."

She cleaned and rebandaged my thumb, and helped me into pajamas with a button-up shirt—the kind I never wear, really—so that it would be easier with my sling. She gave me pain medicine and I went to bed.

I never really caught up on the homework. Mostly I just sat in my classes without a clue what was going on.

Every morning when I got to school, Amanda was waiting. Waiting to make me miserable. She called me and Franklin names, which never seemed to bother him the way it bothered me. She wrecked my lunch, and when I told Mrs. Wakefield about it again, she still didn't seem to care. She considered it part of learning to share the locker, told me that I couldn't switch and I needed to learn to get along with my partner.

It became harder and harder just to get to school.

One morning, after rushing to wash my face and brush my teeth with one hand, I left with only a few minutes to catch the bus. I had to hurry, but instead, my steps got smaller and smaller, and slower and slower. By the time I got to the bus stop, nobody was there.

I couldn't stand at the bus stop all day, so I turned around and went back home.

When Aunt Bessie heard the front door open, she came from the kitchen to see who it was. She was already dressed in her catering clothes. "What happened?"

"I missed the bus."

"How did that happen?"

I shrugged. "I didn't get there in time."

"I have a tasting this morning. . . ." Aunt Bessie seemed pretty stressed out by my reappearance. She sighed. "Get in the car. I'll take you."

"I'm sorry," I said. "It was an accident."

That first morning, we all thought it was an accident.

Feeling Stuck

When you get to the bus stop in the morning and nobody's there, it means one of three things:

(1) You missed the bus.

(2) It's Saturday, but you forgot.

(3) School has been miraculously canceled, but no one told you.

Who am I kidding? I missed the bus. Again.

Today there wasn't actually *no one* at the bus stop. Franklin was there, sitting by the side of the road, knees pulled up, baseball cap and backpack on. When he was crunched up like that with his head down, you couldn't see his pale hair or pale skin or pale blue eyes, or his faded freckles.

If you get to the bus stop in the morning and just Franklin is there, it means one of two things:

(1) Franklin missed the bus, too.

(2) Franklin was there when the bus came, but you weren't, so he waited to keep you company.

Franklin's a good friend that way. Not that we talk about things like that. How Franklin would miss school just to make sure I'm okay. If he got in trouble—well, that was his choice, wasn't it? He didn't have to wait for me.

"Hi, dorkus," I greeted him.

"Hi, Elise," he answered, ignoring the "dorkus." That was new, the name-calling. Everyone in middle school threw around hurtful names like they were meaningless, so why shouldn't I? Franklin hadn't picked up the habit, but he didn't seem offended by it.

"You don't have your sling or your bandage."

"Yesterday the doctor said I didn't have to wear them anymore. He said kids heal pretty fast."

I sat down as Franklin examined his watch, with its big navy face and large white numbers.

"Damage?" I asked.

"Bus comes—seven-forty-eight. School starts—eight-fifteen. Now—eight-twenty-four."

"Dung cookies."

After attendance in the morning, if you aren't there, and no one from home has reported your absence, the school calls your house. That's how I always get found out. After that first morning, I never felt good trudging home. It seemed like this happened a lot, although I wasn't sure how many times. Five, maybe?

Sure enough, it was only a few minutes—"eight-thirty," Franklin reported—until Uncle Hugh came puffing up the hill on his bike. We watched him pedal in silence, his cheeks turning red above his white beard. His beige button-up shirt and tan shorts billowed as the wind caught them. Finally, he was close enough to stop and talk to us without having to shout. He said, "Hop on, Cricket."

I still fit, sort of, in the basket on the front of Uncle Hugh's bike. The basket digs into the backs of my legs and they swing around as we go, but sitting sideways is okay.

I sighed and climbed into the basket. Instead of continuing up the road to school, Uncle Hugh turned around.

"Where are we going?" I asked.

"Home," Uncle Hugh said. "You too, Franklin, I spoke with your mother."

Franklin trotted along with us. With me in the basket, Uncle Hugh was moving very slowly, pedaling just fast enough to keep us from tipping over.

"Why don't you let me walk with Franklin?" I asked. I might have been a toddler strapped into a plastic seat.

"This way," said Uncle Hugh, "I can keep an eye on where you're going."

Uncle Hugh didn't seem angry as he parked the bike and gave me a hand hopping out of the basket, but he didn't say anything as he turned and walked into the house.

I looked at Franklin, who shrugged. We hurried after Uncle Hugh. He led us into the kitchen. He opened three cream sodas and set the bottles on the table. Franklin and I dropped our backpacks and sat down.

Uncle Hugh took a long drink.

"Listen, Cricket," he started. "We've had very few problems as you've grown up, would you agree?"

"I guess so."

"You're about to be twelve next week."

"I know."

"I think that we have suddenly come to a problem."

"About me turning twelve?"

"Turning twelve is no problem. But you are starting to have more responsibility, right?"

I shrugged.

Uncle Hugh addressed Franklin. "Are you not expected to be more responsible, now that you're in middle school?"

"Well . . ." Franklin put down the bottle he'd been slurping from. "We have to get to our classes on our own and remember our homework and books and supplies."

I rolled my eyes.

"That was my impression, too," Uncle Hugh said. "Now, my dear Elise, you have me quite worried. How are you to learn to be responsible to get to your own classes and remember all your homework and books if you can't even get to school?"

He waited. I looked down at the soda bottle I was twisting in my hands. "I don't know."

"Franklin, how long have you been in sixth grade?"

"Three weeks and three days."

"Right. Cricket, you missed the bus on six different mornings. That's a lot. Franklin, how many minutes does it take to walk from here to the bus stop?"

"Six and a half."

Uncle Hugh nodded. "According to Bess, Elise, you weren't late when you had breakfast, and you left with twenty minutes to get to the bus. So something happened on the way to the bus that took longer than it should have."

I didn't know how to explain how lately I had had more thoughts than ever before whirring through my head and sometimes when I stopped to think about them I lost track of time. Or how Aunt Bessie didn't know that I'd left my math book and homework in my room and had to go back for them. Or how it was easy to drag my feet on the way to school because it wasn't like anyone there besides Franklin even cared that I existed.

Uncle Hugh seemed to soften as I took longer and longer to figure out what to say. Franklin finished his drink and wiped his mouth on his sleeve. "Can I have another soda, Uncle Hugh?"

"Don't be ridiculous," Uncle Hugh said. "It's nine in the morning. Your mother will have me shot. Have some water."

Franklin shrugged and got a glass of water.

A car honked outside.

"That's your mother," Uncle Hugh said. "She's going to take you to school. Get your stuff."

Franklin swung his backpack on. "Elise, you coming?"

"No, don't worry," said Uncle Hugh. When Franklin had left, he said, "You're going to stay home, catch up on some of your work, and figure this out. There must be a reason why you don't want to go."

Was Franklin's mother going to be mad at him? She never seems to get mad about anything.

"Are you or Aunt Bessie going to start walking me to the bus stop and putting me on the bus?" I asked.

"What would you learn then? What would be different?"

"Nothing."

Uncle Hugh isn't really the mad type, either. He's the let's-learn-something-from-this type.

"First, head to your room. You're not being punished. I just want you to do some thinking in your own space, okay?"

Soon Aunt Bessie slipped into my room and shut the door.

"Hugh told me he wants to talk to you and I thought, *Men can be so obtuse sometimes*, so I decided to come in myself to see if you wanted a woman to talk to."

I laughed. "Aunt Bessie! It's nothing like that!"

"That's a relief," she said, sitting down on my bed with me. "But still, why talk to men at all when girls are just such better listeners?"

I put my head on her soft shoulder. Aunt Bessie's the best.

"Now," she said, "what's keeping you from getting to school?"

"I don't know."

"Teachers?"

"Maybe. None of them ever call on me. No one holds up my work and says to the rest of the class, 'Your work should be like this!' None of them give me check-pluses, just plain old checks. They all think I'm stupid."

"You aren't stupid," Aunt Bessie said. "But you are going

from a small school, where all your teachers knew you, to a big school, and it's a lot harder to stand out. What about friends?"

"What friends?"

"Come now, Lise, you have friends."

"I don't. Most of the kids from my old school are hanging out with other people or they're in different classes, so I don't see them. I was never really friends with any of them anyway."

"You have Franklin."

"Lot of good he is."

"Has something happened with Franklin?"

"No," I said.

No one likes me because I'm friends with that dweebus Franklin. He makes me look like a baby.

"It's not fair," I said out loud.

"What's not, sweetie?"

It wasn't fair for no one to like me because I'm friends with Franklin. I can not-like Franklin sometimes if I want to, but it's not right for anyone else to not-like Franklin; they don't even know him. And it's definitely not fair for them to not-like me because of him. Not fair.

Really, though, the worst thing would be if they didn't like me because of me. Maybe I was a baby.

I was trying to do my late math homework when a car came down the driveway, so I went out on the front porch and leaned on the railing. Annie parked the car, got out, and waved. *"Hello!"*

I lifted one of my elbows enough to wave back.

Aunt Bessie came flying out of the front door.

"Annie!" She ran down the steps to hug Annie. I always thought it was funny that Aunt Bessie had a sister who was almost twenty years younger.

"Elise! Aren't you going to come down here and welcome our family?" Aunt Bessie called up to me.

I walked slowly off the porch.

Annie opened the backseat and Aunt Bessie swooped in, unbuckling the baby and lifting her from the car. Then she started cooing. Ava let out a happy shriek. She looked pretty cute. I didn't go anywhere near her.

"How are you, Elise?" Annie asked, putting an arm around me. Her eyes were on the baby. I'd never seen anyone look so lovingly at anything.

"All right."

"You can hold her, too, if you like. Let's get her inside, though, Bess; she'll need to be fed. She'll get cranky soon."

"Of course, of course," Aunt Bessie said. She started moving toward the porch with Ava. "Are you hungry?" she asked in a high-pitched voice. "Are you hungry? Yes? Yes, you are?" She called back, "Elise, help Annie with her things!"

I guess Aunt Bessie had forgotten about my bum thumb.

Annie's trunk was packed full. She started pulling luggage out. I grabbed the handle of a duffel bag with my left hand.

"Look at your long hair!" she exclaimed. "How beautiful!"

"I'm thinking of cutting it," I said. My hair is over three feet long. I know because Franklin measured it for me, with a ruler.

"What are you doing home at this time of day?"

"Don't ask."

"Okay. I'm glad you're home today to greet me, whatever the reason. I'm so excited to be here with you," Annie said. "You'll get to be like Ava's big sister. I know you'll just love her."

What's there to love about a baby? They just cry and make messes.

I hauled Annie's things into the extra downstairs bedroom while she nursed Ava in the living room. That was something I didn't want to see. It took about five trips to carry all the bags because I only used my good hand. When that was done, Uncle Hugh showed up with a crib, a changing table, and a special set of plastic drawers. I helped him set up all that stuff as much as I could considering my thumb. It took ages. Uncle Hugh left for a minute, but I was still looking at the new furniture when Annie came into the room, without Ava.

"Where's the baby?"

"She's sleeping. Bess is holding her. Thank you for your help in here." Annie started to move things around the room. "There." She wiped her forehead when everything was in place. "We'll get Ava and see how she likes her new bed. Do you want to hold her?"

"No thanks," I said. "My hands are dirty from putting all that stuff together."

"Elise, I need you!" Uncle Hugh called.

"Gotta go."

Phew.

I found Uncle Hugh on the porch.

"How's your day going?" he asked.

"Uh, fine, we just set up all that furniture together."

"I mean your thinking-about-school day."

"Oh, that." I sat down on the steps. "I guess that's fine, too."

"Did you figure anything out?"

"Not really."

"So you wasted the day?"

"Don't worry. I would have wasted it at school anyway."

Uncle Hugh nearly turned purple. I'd really done it now.

"I'm sorry," I said right away.

"Go to your room. Now. You will make a list of your responsibilities with regards to school. I will be there in twenty minutes to read it."

I didn't need telling twice.

Right on time, Uncle Hugh knocked and opened my door.

"Hello, Cricket."

"Hello, Uncle," I replied from my desk, bent over the paper I was writing on.

Uncle Hugh pulled up a chair. He seemed to have calmed down a lot. "So, what have you come up with?"

"Only three things."

"Good, let's hear them."

"One, get to the bus on time. Two, do my homework. Three, bring the homework to school."

"Two and three are separate things?"

"Yes."

"Ah. Nothing else? Nothing like: remember my gym clothes?"

"I keep them in my locker so I always have them."

"Okay. If these are your main responsibilities, we will use them to set a couple goals. Can you, for one week, make it to the bus every day? Hand in every assignment?"

"I'll try."

"Then we'll set new ones. Reach for a little at a time."

He had me write down the goals, put the date at the top, and tape them to my desk.

School must have ended, because Franklin showed up on the porch. He wasn't being noisy, Franklin never was, but I hurried out and shushed him. "The baby's sleeping. Be quiet."

"Annie and Ava are here?"

"Yep. And we have to be very quiet, so you'd better go."

"I just got here."

"Okay, fine, you can stay. But don't make a sound." I let him in.

"Can I see the baby?" he asked.

"No, she's sleeping."

Annie showed up beside us in the living room. "It's okay, you can peek in."

"No thanks," I said.

"I've never seen a baby up close," Franklin protested.

"You'll see her later. She'll be here every day."

"Ignore Elise, Franklin, and come see her if you want to." Annie led Franklin to her room, and I tromped along, not wanting to be left behind. I stayed in the doorway while Annie and Franklin stood over the crib.

"How old is she?"

"Five months."

"She looks nice."

"Yeah, she does."

We backed up into the hallway and Annie left the door open just a tiny bit. "I want to be able to hear if she wakes up."

"Come on, Franklin," I said. I led him into my room and closed the door.

"Why don't you like the baby?" he asked.

"Who says I don't?"

"You're like, *afraid*, of the baby."

"Babies are boring."

Babies make me nervous. If they're screaming because something is wrong, they can't tell you what to do about it. I'm afraid I'll break them when I touch them. And they make me think of my mother.

Franklin shrugged and reached into his backpack. "I brought your homework. There's tons!"

"Great," I said, taking the stack of books and papers. "How'd you get in my locker?"

"Combination: fifteen-seventeen-seven."

"How do you know that?"

"I watched you do it once and remembered in case I ever needed to get in there. And look, I did."

"Doofus. Anything interesting happen at school today?"

"We learned about magnets in science. We got to play with little metal shavings and watch them collect on a horseshoe magnet."

"No, I mean, with people at school."

"Not that I know of."

Who'd he sit with at lunch? Probably Diana from the bus, with her cat sweaters and gymp key chains and plastic thermos of chocolate milk. I hated it when he sat with Diana.

Franklin settled in at my desk without mentioning the new goals taped there, opened his math book, and labeled his paper. "Aren't you going to start?"

"Yeah, sure." I got out my science book and the worksheet. "Will you help me with the stuff I missed in class? I don't really know that much about magnets."

"Okay," Franklin said. "I was thinking, since we sometimes do our homework together, maybe we could split the books we bring home, so our bags aren't that heavy."

"Good thinking." I sat down on my bed and opened the science book in my lap. "But I never know where my stuff is. You'd end up not able to do your homework if I forgot something."

Franklin nodded. "Can I have a snack?"

I shrugged. "Go get something." I should have gone with him, after he was being nice about the homework stuff, but sometimes it feels like he just comes here to eat.

Franklin headed to the kitchen. I leaned my head back

against the wall. Maybe things would be different when my birthday came. Maybe I'd automatically seem older, cooler, less of a baby. Maybe I'd be smarter and schoolwork would be easier.

Maybe things would be different when I was twelve.

I Make It to School

The next day I made it to the bus on time.

Amanda got to our locker first, like every morning, because she doesn't take the bus.

"Where's your boyfriend?"

"He's not my boyfriend." I reached up to put my lunch on the top shelf.

Amanda stopped me. "My lunch is up there. Put yours in the main section." She took my bag and tossed it onto the pile of books below. "Guess I don't need these." She dropped the rest of her books into the locker, squishing my lunch.

I was still staring at her when her crew of three girls showed up. I had learned their names were Kate, Lindsay, and Caroline, and all four of them came from the same elementary school. Amanda never let anyone, her friends or Franklin, see the lunch-smashing.

Kate and Lindsay were careful not to make eye contact with me. Caroline glanced at me, but then looked away.

The bell rang.

The four girls started to walk toward class.

From down the hall, Franklin called, "Elise! Come on!"

He was running through kids with his arms full of books. Then he slammed into an eighth grader and toppled over backward.

Amanda, Kate, and Lindsay laughed hysterically. Caroline caught my eye again. Franklin didn't notice that a whole bunch of people were laughing at him.

I had two choices: I could help Franklin up and get teased and laughed at again, or ignore him.

I left Franklin fumbling for books, trying to keep his balance with his backpack on, and followed Caroline to class.

Franklin showed up late, pink and out of breath, and slipped into the seat next to me. He always comes right back to me. Like a puppy-dog friend.

Mrs. Wakefield had corrected our paragraphs from the day before. "Caroline, will you read yours?"

Caroline walked to the front and read in a clear voice. It was about the ocean. It had full sentences, but it sounded like poetry.

When Caroline sat back down, Mrs. Wakefield commented on how she really liked her descriptions. How you could feel the wet sand under your toes and hear the waves rolling in. Then she returned everyone else's papers. My paper wasn't smooth like Caroline's. It had jaggy edges because I had ripped it out of a notebook, and there was a tear in the paper where I had erased too hard. Mrs. Wakefield had written only a check on it.

Amanda, Kate, and Lindsay didn't seem to like that Caroline got attention for her essay. They didn't say good job or anything. I peeked sideways; Caroline was looking down at her paper. Her ears were pink underneath her shiny, shoulder-length hair, which was pulled back with a headband.

"I liked your paragraph," I whispered. She produced a tiny smile.

Mrs. Wakefield started talking about nouns and verbs and nothing, and I doodled over the check mark on my paper with a red pen until the check mark was an A. An A+.

After school we went to Leonard's, and Franklin let me go talk to Leonard by myself for a few minutes, as usual. I breathed in deeply to soak in that great hardware-store smell before I found him shelving stuff.

"Hi, Leonard."

"Hey, Elise. How's school? You seem to have barely any time to come by the old shop anymore."

I shrugged. "It's busy." *And awful,* I added in my head.

"What's that?"

"What's what?"

"The part after busy?"

"I didn't say anything."

"But you *thought* something after busy."

"It's awful. That's what I thought. School is still awful."

"Want to tell me about it?"

"No, I don't." It wasn't so much that I didn't want to tell Leonard, but I saw no reason to bring Amanda into the store.

"You know what we used to do, your dad and me?"

"What? Go up to the old lake?"

"That's right. Go up to the old lake." Leonard was always

talking about how he and Dad did that. "Get away from life for a while, talk about things. Nothing a trip there couldn't solve. Everything always seemed a bit better when we came back."

I'd heard about the old lake a million gazillion times. Leonard really seemed to like to talk about it, so I always let him. But this time, him mentioning a place where you took your troubles to talk about them—it seemed like he had been reading my mind again.

"Sounds like a great place."

"It was, it was." Then he changed the subject. "Ready to turn a year older?"

"So ready. You're coming, right? To my birthday?"

"Of course. Would I miss the biggest sloppy-joe fest of the year?"

"Okay, good."

"And don't forget," Leonard said, "just because you're growing up doesn't mean you don't have to come by to visit your old friend."

"I won't forget."

On Saturday afternoon I headed into the kitchen. Aunt Bessie didn't have a job, so that made this our time.

On the counter were a butternut squash, a banana, an avocado, and a bag of apples. I didn't think they went together.

"What are we making?"

"Baby food."

"Like, for Ava?"

"Yes! Isn't it exciting?"

"I thought she didn't eat food, just milk."

"Well, the doctor said she still needs all that milk, but that she can be introduced to certain foods now. We're making her lots of things because we aren't sure what she likes best. She's tried most of them before, but the avocado will be new today."

"How much can she eat?"

"A spoonful."

"A spoonful? All this for a spoonful?"

"Well, *she* doesn't even know what she likes. So we'll let her taste things." She was talking about Ava like she was a person with opinions, not a blob. "Here. Why don't you peel all the apples? We'll make some into applesauce. I'll get to work on the squash."

Cooking time with Aunt Bessie was supposed to be about me and her, not about a baby who happened to live in our house. I didn't talk as I peeled the apple skins into a big container. The applesauce took a long time to make and a lot of arm strength to turn the crank of the strainer over and over and over with my left hand. The avocado and the banana got mushed up at the last minute, because they didn't need to be cooked.

Life with Annie and Ava had been pretty peaceful so far. Their room was on the first floor, like mine, but on the opposite side of the house, so I didn't hear Ava crying too much. And I was at school for most of the day. Ava usually sat on the floor in her baby carrier seat at dinner, and often she just fell asleep, because it must be boring to watch people eat. She might not even have been able to see us from down there.

Franklin looked up how far babies can see and told me that most babies don't develop full visual capabilities until about eight months. Ava had a couple months to go.

Annie and Ava were sharing my bathroom, and it had a lot of new things in it. Like a little yellow bathtub stored in the big bathtub that I had to move out whenever I wanted to take a shower. And sometimes Ava's tiny bibs or clothes hung on the towel racks. Luckily the changing table was nowhere near me or my room.

Mostly I just didn't pay attention to Ava. Everything she did seemed cute to the others, and every little cry was something to take care of.

Finally, the food was ready. Annie brought Ava in, sat her up in a high chair, and buttoned a soft bib around her neck.

"Are you ready?" Annie asked her in a sweet, tiny, just-for-Ava voice. "Are you ready to try some food?"

Ava smiled a gurgly smile.

We pulled up three chairs around the high chair. We each had a little container of food and a plastic-coated baby spoon.

"Want to go first?" Annie invited me.

"She's your baby," I said.

Aunt Bessie nodded. Annie took a tiny spoonful of mashed squash and pressed it to Ava's lips.

Ava looked confused, stuck her tongue out, and pushed the food away.

We laughed. Which made Ava widen her eyes and smile back, wondering what clever thing she'd done now.

The story was the same for applesauce, banana . . . then it was my turn with the avocado.

A little flutter of nerves ran through my belly when I lifted the spoon for her. I tried to be extra gentle as I pushed the spoon past her lips and set the little plop of avocado there. I realized it was the closest contact I'd had with Ava. We were only as far apart as a mini, made-for-babies spoon.

The avocado went down better. At least, less of it came back out. She seemed to be thinking about it.

"Ooh, I think she liked that best so far," Annie said. "Try it again."

I fed Ava another spoon-tip of avocado.

By the end, it seemed that she liked banana best. But who knew, really? She was a baby.

When the feeding was over, Ava hadn't eaten more than the spoonful Aunt Bessie had predicted, but she was covered in food.

"The bib is all wrecked," I said as Annie wiped Ava's face with it.

"We'll wash it. It may stain, but that's what it's for. Then one day, we'll just toss it away," Aunt Bessie said.

"Sometimes I think I'll become very attached to these baby things and try to keep them all," Annie admitted.

"It's okay to keep some things. I have a lot of Elise's things upstairs in the attic."

It was true. We took them out and looked at them sometimes. Not lately, though. Not since Little Miss Baby-Pants arrived.

I wondered if Aunt Bessie was going to offer to give my things to Ava, but she didn't. Maybe old things like that are off-limits, like stuff in museums.

"Maybe you can show me sometime, Elise," Annie said, lifting Ava out of the high chair.

"Yeah, maybe," I said.

Annie took Ava to give her a bath. There was avocado stuck in her fluffy hair.

"Should we make our dinner?" I asked Aunt Bessie. Maybe now would be our time together.

"It's already made. I've had pork in the oven this whole time. And you made the applesauce."

I was setting the table when Annie came back with Ava, squeaky-clean and wearing pajamas. Not that daytime baby clothes and nighttime baby clothes are all that different. The pj's have feet on them and the daytime clothes don't. Annie buckled Ava into her carrier on the floor as Uncle Hugh came in.

"I've got a surprise for you, Annie. Cricket, will you come hold the door?"

I held the screen door wide open while Uncle Hugh carried in a large piece of beautiful blue furniture and set it on its rockers on the tile floor. My mouth dropped open.

"There," he said proudly. "I thought it would be nice for you and Ava. It's good and sturdy. We can put it right in your room."

"Oh, thank you!" Annie hugged Uncle Hugh. He laughed as he patted her back.

I shut the door. Uncle Hugh hadn't known I'd wanted the chair; I never said anything about it. I knew it wasn't fair for me to be mad, but I was.

7

I Turn Twelve

My birthday started off okay. I got all my homework into my backpack and made it to the bus on time. Franklin gave me a chocolate cupcake.

"I made two dozen," he said. "Only this one looked nice." The chocolate frosting had big finger dents.

"Thanks." I licked some of the frosting off my own finger, to show him that I wasn't grossed out.

But really, I think I was.

Franklin came over in the afternoon, wearing his bicycle helmet.

"What's that for?" I asked.

"Protection."

"From what?"

"Cousins."

Once when we were little my cousins Jake and Alec had hit Franklin with mud balls until he went home crying. Another time they hung him from the porch roof by his ankles— and forgot about him.

"Baby," I said. "They don't do stuff like that anymore." Jake and Alec were seventeen and fifteen now. It would be a surprise if they stayed through dinner, let alone had time to "play."

"Still," Franklin said. "What's for dinner? Am I allergic to it?"

"Not unless you're suddenly allergic to hamburger buns," I said. "It's sloppy joes."

I *always* have sloppy joes on my birthday. Franklin should have known that. But he was just being careful, so I added, more nicely, "The cake and frosting are safe, too. Come see."

We walked into the kitchen, where Annie was pacing with Ava and talking to Aunt Bessie, who was frosting my cake.

"Blue again?" asked Franklin.

"I like blue," I said. "It looks good and tastes good." He should talk, after all those blue slushies. I scooped a glob from the frosting bowl.

Aunt Bessie smacked my wrist, but she wasn't angry. "Get out of here!"

Franklin and I went back outside. He chose a perch on a low branch of a tree.

"Sure it's safe up there?" I teased him.

"It's three feet off the ground," he said. "If I fell it would be only minor injuries. But if the cousins sneak up on me . . . the consequences could be disastrous."

"They can't sneak up on you," I said. "They're coming in a car."

Leonard showed up and gave me a kiss on the forehead. "Where's your uncle?"

"Probably his workshop."

He headed there.

"You get your birthday letter tonight," Franklin reminded me.

"I know," I said.

"Excited?"

"A little."

After a while, my cousins' car pulled into our long driveway. Aunt Sally jumped out first.

"Look at you, girl! All grown up!" she shrieked as she gave me a hug. "There's a baby in the house, right? I'm dying to meet her!" She ran up the porch steps. Whose birthday was it, anyway?

Uncle Beau hugged me, and Jake rubbed his fist against my head.

Franklin dropped out of his tree-perch.

"What's with the helmet?" Jake asked.

"I'm protecting my cranium from *you*," Franklin said.

"Great," said Alec, pounding on the top of the helmet. Franklin held it down tight with both hands.

I rolled my eyes. "Come on, we can go eat."

Because of the sloppy joes, we were going to eat in the kitchen instead of the dining room. Uncle Hugh had already brought in extra chairs, so everything was ready.

The sloppy joes were awesome, as always. Two silent competitions began between those who wanted to be the sloppiest and those who wanted to be the neatest. All the boys were a total mess. Aunt Bessie and Aunt Sally took tiny bites, but Annie let sauce gush out the back of her hamburger bun and left some on her chin. That made me laugh. Then the messy-competition got loud with laughter. Alec dipped his fingers in the red sauce and made war-paint streaks on his cheeks. Franklin had sauce all over his face and hands, but I don't think it was on purpose. Ava stayed in her carrier seat on the floor and no one paid any attention to her, for once.

After we all cleaned up, it was time for cake and presents. I got . . .

. . . a fifty-dollar gift certificate to the movie store from Aunt Sally and Uncle Beau.

. . . a One Free Day Trip pass from Leonard to anywhere I wanted. What came to mind right away was the amusement park, but it was October, so it was closed until spring. I'd have to think about where I wanted to go.

. . . an easy cookbook from Aunt Bessie. She wrote in it: *We can learn the recipes and spend more time together in the kitchen!*

. . . a goal journal from Uncle Hugh. It has pages in it where you can write the goal at the top, how you plan to achieve it, steps you've taken, and then the date of achievement on the bottom. He smiled at me when I opened it.

. . . a book of knot-tying techniques from Franklin. "You need to improve your skills. Then," he added in a whisper, "you can hang your lunch from a hook in your locker instead of letting Amanda squish it, and she won't be able to get it off." It sounded neat to practice knots, but maybe not in my locker. Amanda might make a big deal of that. Franklin's bright ideas could get me made fun of again.

I took the birthday ribbon from Aunt Bessie's present and looped it through my hair around my ponytail. The table was strewn with plates of half-eaten cake and wrapping paper, but my birthday wasn't over yet. I would get my letter at bedtime. But first I said goodbye to my guests.

Franklin was last to go. His mom came to pick him up.

"You have sloppy-joe sauce on your ear," I said as we stood on the porch.

"Oh." Franklin tried to wipe it, but he didn't know where it was. I licked my thumb and wiped it off for him. "See you tomorrow," he said. "Don't forget to start practicing those knots."

"I won't," I said.

I carefully washed any last traces of sloppy joe and blue frosting off my face and put on my pajamas. I got in bed, but sat up, waiting.

Aunt Bessie slipped into my room and handed me an envelope.

It said: *Elise, 12.*

"Elise?" Aunt Bessie said gently, drawing my attention away from the unopened envelope. "It's the last one. We didn't tell you. We didn't want you counting down."

It hadn't occurred to me that the letters would run out. It would be weird without one next year. I thought there would be one every birthday, for my whole life.

Maybe that would be a lot of letters.

"That's okay."

"Do you want me to stay?" Aunt Bessie asked.

"No, you don't need to."

"Good night, Cricket. Happy birthday." Aunt Bessie kissed me on the forehead, left my room, and shut the door.

For a few minutes I just held the letter. Then I slid my finger under the flap. After so many years, the glue had mostly disappeared, so it opened easily. I pulled out the plain sheet of paper, unfolded it, and began to read:

Dear Elise,

Today you had a lovely time playing outside in the rain. You just got a new pair of bright red boots and a matching raincoat, so it was nearly impossible to keep you inside. There were ducks in the pond who ruffled their feathers a bit when you tried to catch them, but they didn't fly away, so they must have liked playing with you.

How grown up you must be now. I wonder if you are wearing your hair long and dark like your mother's.

I don't know what we are to do without each other, but by the time you read this, you will have been managing on your own for quite a while. Have you been looking after my brother? He needs some taking care of from time to time, and now you're old enough to tell him what's what. You better be listening to him, too! He has a good heart, your Uncle Hugh.

This letter will be my last to you, but

please don't be sad. I'm leaving something else for you, to discover and unlock when you are ready. Remember that while others can help, in great part we mold ourselves.

I miss you so much already, thinking of not being there with you on this happy day. But we will find each other again, I promise, even if not in this life, and when we do meet again, I know you will be the best Elise that you can be.

All my love,
Daddy

I ran my fingers through my hair, all the way to its ends. I was glad I hadn't cut it. I wondered if the dark color of Mom's hair he mentioned really was the same color as mine—a deep, chocolaty brown.

I don't have any memories of Mom, and only a few of Dad—mostly what Uncle Hugh, Aunt Bessie, and Leonard tell me. Which is enough, usually.

My birthday—my first day, and Mom's last—would be the only day the three of us were all in this world together. It made sense for Dad to commemorate that day with letters.

But what had Dad meant, he was "leaving something else" for me? What would it be? And where was it? And how was I supposed to find it?

The thoughts whirred in my head until they became heavy and dreamlike, and I fell asleep.

8

Being Twelve Is (Unfortunately) Just Like Being Eleven

The curling ribbons from Aunt Bessie's present were still tangled in my hair. My neck hurt. And my eyes felt funny, because everything seemed all green. The light had been on all night.

It was morning; my birthday was over.

I wrapped a sweatshirt blanket around me and stumbled to the kitchen.

"Morning, cupcake." Aunt Bessie hugged me hard, pressing my head into her chest. "Your breakfast is ready." On the table was a plate with an enormous slice of birthday cake and a tall glass of milk.

"Thanks." I started to eat. The cake tasted so good for breakfast.

"Will you be ready to go in twenty minutes?"

Only then did I realize: "I didn't do any of my homework."

"Why not? You knew you were having a party. You should have done it right after school."

"I thought there would be time after everyone left."

"You really should have done it before. Do you need some sort of note?"

I shook my head. "The teachers don't care if it's your birthday. That kind of thing is for first graders."

Just then, Ava started crying. Aunt Bessie bustled off.

I pulled the half-flattened ribbons out of my hair and left them on the table.

Franklin decided to go to an "Interested in Student Government?" meeting during lunch. I was definitely Not Interested, so I headed to the cafeteria on my own for the first time. I wasn't sure where to sit. The lunchroom is big, crowded with kids from all grades, so it doesn't seem like the friendliest of places without your trusted buddy.

One girl was sitting by herself. She looked small enough to be a sixth grader. Maybe she'd be really neat and we could be friends.

"Hi. Can I sit here?"

The girl thought for a minute. "Where's that weird boy you're always with? Would he have to come, too?"

"No," I said, stunned. "And never mind."

I continued to wander the tables until I spotted Caroline eating alone. Just knowing her name made her seem comfortingly familiar. I sat diagonal from her, returned her smile, and took out my pulverized PB&J and bruised apple.

I was just opening my mouth to take a bite when someone announced in my ear, "Move it, Scab-Picker." Amanda was standing there, surrounded, as usual, by sidekicks.

I shut my mouth, missing the sandwich. I didn't want to

find out what she'd say next if I stuck around, but didn't want to give in entirely. I slid my lunch to the last spot at the table and bumped down the seats. When I picked up my sandwich, Amanda hollered, "I said move it, Scabular. We don't want you at our table."

My throat felt like I was choking. I'm not a crier; I could count on one hand the number of times I remembered crying. But it seemed that if I opened my mouth, I might start to cry right there in the lunchroom. That would be even worse than scabby legs or bandaged hands.

I put my sandwich in my bag and moved three tables over near some kids I didn't know.

Maybe they didn't know I was a loser.

They didn't even look at me.

"I finished my homework," Franklin announced when he showed up in my room that afternoon.

"Good for you, dorkus," I said. "I didn't even start." I had been lying in my bed, staring at the ceiling.

"Want to play Knights?"

I looked at the smooth white patches of skin on my healed legs. I thought about lunch, and how those scabs were going to stick with me forever now. About how there'd been another silly-looking injury the very next week. Maybe there was a tiny chance that people would forget if I was more careful.

"No."

"Oh, okay," Franklin said. "What do you want to do? We could play Robbers, or tag, or—"

"I don't want to play," I said. I added, in a whisper, "I don't want to play ever again."

"Why not?"

"We're too old."

"Since when? I don't remember any rules about that."

"Well, there are. I just don't want to anymore."

"Want to do something else, then?"

"Not really."

Franklin crouched down and started tracing marks with his fingers along the floorboards.

About ten minutes later, he finally said, "How many floorboards do you think there are?"

"I don't know."

"We could probably figure it out. . . . Oh, I know! I totally forgot. I'll be back in a few minutes."

He must have gone all the way home, because twenty minutes later he returned with a cardboard box. Its contents made a shifting sound. "A puzzle. A thousand pieces. I haven't even opened it."

Was a puzzle a cool thing to do? Well, I was pretty sure no telltale injuries could happen from working on it. It was nice of Franklin to think of something like that.

We went to work on the dining room table. The puzzle was of a space shuttle orbiting Earth. Franklin, of course, had a systematic plan.

"First we'll separate things into four piles: edges, black space pieces, white shuttle pieces, and blue and green Earth pieces."

We dumped the pieces out and started sorting. For some reason, I couldn't help sliding separated pieces back into the big pile when Franklin wasn't looking.

In the morning, I hadn't touched my homework. I hadn't studied for the math test or researched for my language arts author's life report or answered the social studies questions.

I figured Franklin could help, but I couldn't listen to more than a minute of his advice for the math test on the bus ride.

". . . then you isolate the variable using inverse operations—"

"Speak English, dorkwad."

"That is English. What's the matter? You're half asleep."

"I had weird dreams all night."

"What did you dream about?"

"Going to school and no one could see me. Being at home and no one could see me."

"I've never had dreams like that."

When Franklin has bad dreams, they must be about living in a world without things to measure with.

When we got to school, Amanda squashed my lunch. I got zeros on most of my homework. I was pretty sure I failed the math test.

The worst thing happened between sixth and seventh periods. I stopped at Franklin's locker with him, and when he opened it a bunch of Star Wars action figures tumbled all over the floor.

A boy named Jason picked up Chewbacca and pretended

that he was attacking his friend. Then he threw Chewbacca at Franklin, who was kneeling to collect his toys. Jason and other kids laughed. "I didn't know we had kindergarten in this building."

I glared at Jason. He lifted his hands in the air and said, "He's your friend."

Despite all that, Franklin decided to keep Chewbacca sticking out of his pocket. It was impossible to forget the whole thing, sitting in Spanish with Chewbacca peering out at me.

On the walk home from the bus I trudged silently next to Franklin. We live in opposite directions, so we started off as if heading to my house, because that was the direction my feet went in automatically.

"Want to come over?" Franklin asked. "I got new movies about the Apollo space missions."

"No thanks."

"You're no fun anymore."

"You're a baby. You don't understand." I threw insults at Franklin all the time these days, but this one came out differently. I spoke softly, barely above a whisper, in a voice that said I meant it.

For the first time, he looked hurt.

"Fine. I'll learn about the space program by myself."

"I don't care about the space program!" I yelled. "And you obviously don't care about me, so go home and watch your stupid movies."

Franklin stared at me like I had hit him. Then he held back the water in his eyes, turned around, and headed home.

I stormed to my own house. This was all Franklin's fault.

• • •

The next day was even *worse*.

Because I hadn't done my homework again, I was in even more trouble. Franklin wasn't speaking to me. Okay, he was *speaking* to me, but not like a friend would. He sat with Diana at lunch. I walked by and overheard her talking about how she watched her gerbil push out a bunch of babies last night. Yeck. I picked a different table. Which was fine, really, because even though you aren't allowed to bring work to lunch, I had snuck in my social studies book and was going to try to finish the questions from yesterday.

I put my heading on the paper and set the book on my lap under the table so it was pretty hidden. I tapped the eraser of my pencil on the pages as I read. I was never going to finish the reading, let alone get to the questions. It was hopeless. Like me.

"There's a better way to do that, you know," a voice said. The voice wasn't mean. It sounded kind.

I looked up to see that Caroline had sat next to me.

"What?"

"You're doing it wrong. There's a better way." She gently took the book and turned to the end of the section. "Read the question first so you know what's important to look for, then skim the text until you find the answer. The answer to the next question will be after it, so go in order. If you sit there and read it, you won't remember the answers, and you'll have to look for them all again anyway."

"Thanks. You're really smart, Caroline."

She shook her head.

"You are," I insisted.

"No, I'm annoying. No one likes it."

She meant her stupid friends didn't like it. "No, it's good to be smart."

"Sometime I wish I weren't." Caroline was quiet, chewing her bologna and cheese sandwich while I wrote down the answer to question one. "Are you okay?" she asked when I was done.

"What do you mean?"

"You seem . . . I don't know, upset or something. And you aren't with Franklin."

"Yeah . . . I have a lot going on," I said.

"What on earth could *you* have going on? Playdates?" Amanda was standing across the table from us. Caroline and I just sat. I don't think Amanda expected us to answer her. She looked at Caroline. "Brennan invited us to sit with his friends. You're coming?"

Caroline shrugged. "I'll see you later, Elise, okay? You need to finish that anyway."

"Bye," I said.

"Why are you talking to *her?*" Amanda asked as they walked away. Caroline didn't respond.

She was so different from Amanda. How had they become friends in the first place?

I finished most of the questions, so I'd be able to hand in *something*. But I didn't have time to eat. Not that pulverized peanut butter and jelly is that appetizing.

• • •

"Cricket?" Uncle Hugh pushed open the door to my room. I had my science book open, but I was staring at my long list of late homework. I would never finish it. "It's time for another soda."

I followed him to the kitchen, where he had drinks ready. I opened mine.

"One of your teachers called."

"Oh goody." I couldn't meet his eye.

"It seems like you haven't been doing any work lately."

"That's not true. I did some. I've been trying."

Uncle Hugh twisted the bottle in his hand and started to peel off the label. "I got a call from Franklin's mother, too. Apparently, Franklin is all upset that you hate him and he doesn't know why."

"The worm," I said. "He should know why."

"You hate him?"

"No, I don't hate him. He just made me mad."

"So as far as I can tell, you're getting to school, right?"

"Yes."

"But things don't really seem to be any better."

"Why would they be any better?" I asked quietly. "Nothing's changed."

"Well, sometimes things don't change on their own. Sometimes we have to change them."

"I don't know what to do."

"Try little things, like we talked about before. Homework

first. Be patient with Franklin; he's still the same friend to you he's always been. What else is going on?"

"Nothing."

"Then start with the homework and Franklin. And spend more time with us, too. You haven't been in the kitchen with Bessie much lately. Get to know Annie and Ava. We all love you already; you don't have to prove anything to us."

I nodded. I hadn't been hanging out with Aunt Bessie because I could never get her to myself. I didn't want to spend extra time with Annie and Ava. Especially not since Annie had been talking with Bessie about working for her catering company. Would I get any time with Aunt Bessie if that happened?

"Did I see you with a big list of homework before I interrupted you?"

"Yes."

"Go get it. And all your books and stuff, too. We'll set you up here in the kitchen. It'll be easier. We'll be here."

That night, I stayed up wondering about what Uncle Hugh had said about how things don't change on their own. I'd been waiting to be twelve like I would miraculously be different. But I wasn't.

Then I thought about Dad's letter. He'd written something kind of like what Uncle Hugh had said. I got the letter and found the spot again: "in great part we mold ourselves."

Then I was stuck on something else: on the words "discover and unlock."

Unlock, unlock, unlock, unlock . . .

All of a sudden I remembered it—the key in Uncle Hugh's workshop.

Was that what Dad meant by unlock? I would literally *unlock* something?

But *what*? What was locked?

As I got sleepier, I pictured things that were locked with keys. Houses. Old trunks. Cars. Padlocks. Doors.

I sat up in bed, suddenly awake.

There were *eight* locked doors upstairs in the barn. *Eight* of them!

Could *those* be for *me*?

But the feeling of excitement disappeared almost as quickly as it had come.

Those doors were off-limits. They always had been.

I checked Dad's letter again: "discover and unlock *when you are ready.*"

Maybe I just hadn't been ready.

But now I was ready for *something* to be different. For *anything* to be different.

Tomorrow I'd take a chance and see what that key opened up.

It had my name on it, after all.

Part II

The First Little, Secret Room

After a night of not much sleeping, I woke up, raced through the world's shortest shower, and found just what I wanted to find: Uncle Hugh and Aunt Bessie having morning coffee in the kitchen.

"You already have your backpack on, ready to go!" Aunt Bessie seemed very surprised to see me. She and Uncle Hugh were still in bathrobes. Even on days when neither of them is going to leave the house, they both insist on getting dressed before eight a.m.

"Yeah," I said, swinging my wet ponytail over my shoulder as I grabbed a scone from a plateful on the table. "You know . . . I'm trying not to be late anymore."

"Good for you, Cricket," Uncle Hugh said.

"Well, bye!"

"Well, bye," echoed Uncle Hugh. I headed out the front door.

I had time to visit the barn without worrying that Uncle Hugh would be working there or that Aunt Bessie would be out loading up the van or watering her flowers.

I ran across the driveway and into the barn. I didn't think

I'd been spotted. I darted to the little room where I'd seen the key. Still there!

A shiver of excitement ran through me as I lifted the key.

I wasn't going to use the key right away, I decided, slipping it into the pocket of my jeans. I was going to hold on to it, just for the day. For now, the key had infinite possibilities. It would be nice to have a day of infinite possibilities.

School was okay. There was the usual trouble with Amanda, but most of my homework was done, thanks to Uncle Hugh. Franklin had found some boys to hang out with—the one who shares his locker and his two friends—which hurt less, somehow, than if he'd had lunch with Diana. He and I sat together silently on the bus home. I kind of wanted to tell him about the key, and I even, just a little, wanted him to come with me on a treasure hunt to discover what it unlocked, but something kept me silent. He hadn't been interested in the key when I'd found it, just in making that castle. Why would he be interested now?

At our stop, we headed in separate directions.

Uncle Hugh was out at a customer's house, and Aunt Bessie was inside baking for an event. Perfect, perfect.

I snuck into the barn, left my backpack on the ground floor, fished the key out of my pocket, and held it in my hands.

I slowly walked up the steps. My shoes left prints in the

dust. Uncle Hugh really didn't come up here much. Or maybe he used the elevator.

At the top of the stairs, I took a deep breath and looked at the row of doors. They stood in a tight line, like soldiers at their stations or trees planted to grow up together, seeming not like simple doors but like living things. The breeze that danced through the drafty hallway made it feel like they might even be breathing.

There was nothing to tell me what might be different about each of them. I decided to start with the closest one.

The key didn't fit.

Next door.

It fit.

Already! On the second door. The room *was* for me!

I gave the key a twist, and the door unlocked.

I stood back and pushed it so that it opened wide.

I could see years of dust on the floor. A lot came up in the air, disturbed by the door opening, fuzzy in the yellow afternoon light passing through a single warpy-glass window. I coughed and covered my face with my arm.

I took a few steps inside. The walls on the long sides of the narrow room seemed to be shiny, like glass. I crept closer to look.

The walls were covered in framed pictures, many of the same woman. Some pictures were of a baby, or a girl, or a teenager.

I knew who the woman was. And the baby and the girl and the teenager.

We had pictures of her in the house, but not like this. The ones in the house were there all the time, faded into the background, like wallpaper or furniture. These were meant to be looked at, thought about. I walked up to one, pressed my finger to it. "Mom?"

There were at least a dozen portraits. I stopped and looked at each one carefully.

In one she perches at the top of a slide as a three-year-old. She wears a huge smile, her face framed with soft dark curls. I stayed at this picture for several minutes.

In another she looks almost exactly like me. I looked at my own reflection on the glass to compare it. Maybe she's twelve, too, in the picture.

Then I found one with me in it. You couldn't see me, exactly, but I'm there. She's pregnant. The picture is from the side. She isn't looking at the camera but down, at the bulge of stomach resting on her linked arms. She's looking at me—a me she can't even see—with the same expression that Annie uses to look at Ava.

She'd never even met me—how could she look at me that way?

I heard something crunch under my feet. I was stepping on paper. No, a message.

I picked up the slightly yellowed paper. It said, in typed block letters:

KNOW WHAT YOU COME FROM.

I turned to see if there was anything else in the little room, and there was: a big, comfy chair under the window.

The chair was occupied.

At first I thought the lump was a pillow, but it was a teddy bear. He was missing an eye, his sewn-on bow tie was crooked, and his fur was worn through to threads in several places. But he was a literate bear, because he was holding a note. Sure, the "Elise" on the outside of the folded paper matched the ones on my birthday letters, but the inside of the note said,

> Hello, Elise,
>
>   It's nice to see you again. My name is Miles. I belonged to your mother a long time ago. I was her most special toy. When you were a baby, I sat in your nursery and watched over you while you slept. You never quite took to me like she did (you preferred Bunny-Rabbit), but I knew you both.
>
>   Please take care of me.
>
>   Love,
>   Miles

I remembered Bunny-Rabbit. My favorite soft toy, who had been on several trips through the washing machine and had almost fallen apart. She sat on the top shelf of my closet now, safe.

I picked up Miles, buried my nose in his fur, and breathed in deeply. Miles didn't smell like a person, just an old stuffed bear. I felt silly for expecting more than that. He made me cough because he was so dusty.

When a stuffed bear asks you for help, you can . . . ignore him, check your sanity, or give in.

"Welcome back, Miles," I whispered.

I sat down and held him in my lap while I studied the portraits.

Eventually, I realized that the sun was starting to slip down below the trees. I had to go or Aunt Bessie would start wondering where I was. I brought the note, KNOW WHAT YOU COME FROM, and Miles with me and squeezed them into my backpack, zipped it up, and swung it over my shoulder. I was careful to shut the barn door just as it had been.

On the way out, I was spotted. Annie and Ava were on a walk. Or at least, Annie was walking, holding Ava.

"Hi," I said. She didn't seem to think it was weird for me to come out of the barn.

"Hi, Elise," Annie said. "I just thought Ava would like to see the trees. They're so pretty this time of year."

Ava probably wasn't old enough to understand that she was looking at trees. They would just be red and yellow and orange blobs.

But Annie really *wanted* her to see those things. That had to count for something, didn't it?

And that must be how you learn *trees*, right? Someone points them out to you and calls them *trees*?

I thought about the note from Dad and the pictures and Miles. What exactly was he trying to point out to me?

"Elise?" Annie asked. I had been quiet for too long, I guess.

"Don't you have a stroller?" I asked.

"It doesn't work so well on gravel and grass. We keep it in the car for in town, where there are sidewalks."

"Oh. That's smart."

"We're going in now."

"Me too."

I walked up the porch steps with Annie.

I managed to keep my secret only until bedtime. I had taken Miles out of my backpack. I held him in bed, wondering, letting my thoughts whir. The unfolded note lay in my lap: KNOW WHAT YOU COME FROM.

But Uncle Hugh came in my room. "Just saying good night."

"Oh. Good night, Uncle Hugh."

He sat on my bed. "All your homework done tonight?"

"Some of it."

"Some of it?"

"Okay, *most* of it. I have more reading."

Uncle Hugh noticed my stuffed friend.

"Where did you get that?"

"Do you know who it is?"

"Of course I do," he said. He lifted the bear from my arms

and gave him a gentle squeeze. "Where has he been all these years? Find him in the attic?"

I couldn't decide whether to lie or not. "Not exactly."

Uncle Hugh paused, then had a look of realization. He said, not really to me, "Is it time, already?"

"Time for what?"

"I've been waiting for years, even checking sometimes, waiting for that little key to disappear. Waiting and waiting, but never actually thinking you'd be ready."

"It's been there for years?"

"Oh yes."

"How many?"

"Nine."

"Ever since?"

"Ever since. And a little before, of course."

I nodded.

"You didn't tell me."

"I wasn't supposed to."

We both sat quiet. Uncle Hugh handed back Miles.

Aunt Bessie passed in the hall.

"Bess!" Uncle Hugh called. "Come in here for a minute."

She peeked around the door. "It's late. What's going on?"

Uncle Hugh said, "Our Elise found her key today."

"Oh," Aunt Bessie said, looking fairly shocked. She came in and sat in my desk chair. "Did you . . . use it?"

I held up Miles.

"You did. Was that all? Just Milo?"

"Miles," I corrected.

"Right. Miles."

"Pictures," I said, "of Mom. And a pink chair. And this note." I held the paper out to them. Uncle Hugh took it.

"Well?" I prompted. "Tell me about her."

"Haven't we before?" Aunt Bessie asked.

"Well, sure," I said. "But this is different."

Aunt Bessie nodded. "She was very sweet. She had that pretty long, dark hair she would never cut, and big light-brown eyes that sparkled. She was always smiling and laughing, unless someone was making fun of someone else. She never liked that. I remember when I met her, she talked to me like we had been friends for years: handed me a triple-scoop ice cream cone, sat me down on the porch, and asked me what I really thought of those Bertrand boys."

"What did you say?" Uncle Hugh interrupted, with a sly smile.

"You'll never know." Aunt Bessie wore an equally sly smile.

"Were you kids?" I asked.

"No, grown-ups. She was already with your father, and I was with Hugh. She was a good friend. We grew to be very close."

"What's with the chair?" I asked.

"You said it was pink, right? I'd guess it was your mother's favorite reading chair. She used to like to sit and read in it for hours, even more so when it was nearly time for you to get here. She kept it by the window in her bedroom, where the afternoon light was good for reading. She couldn't go out much then. The doctor thought it would be better for her to stay in bed as much as possible. High-risk pregnancy, he said."

"What about the other rooms?" I asked. "There was only one key, but there are still seven rooms."

"I guess you just can't worry about the other rooms. Maybe you'll get to open them later," Uncle Hugh said.

"But there aren't any more keys for me."

"That doesn't mean the keys don't exist. They're still out there, somewhere."

"Are you sure you want them right away?" Aunt Bessie asked. "Wasn't that enough for now?"

"For today," I said. "But now that I know those are for me, I want to know what's in them."

"Just keep your eyes open. Isn't that how you found this one?"

I nodded.

"How did you put two and two together?" Uncle Hugh asked.

I pointed to the birthday letter on my nightstand.

"You doing okay?"

"Yeah, I'm just tired now."

Aunt Bessie got up and put her hand on Uncle Hugh's shoulder.

"Good night, Cricket," he said. "Sleep well. Your dad loved games, puzzles, and clues. He asked us to keep this secret."

"That's okay," I said. "I needed a surprise."

At school the next day, I thought about Mom, who was kind, and a good friend, and a reader, and somehow brave.

If Dad wanted me to know what I came from, did that

mean I should have those things inside me somewhere? Was that true? I didn't seem to be anything like my mother. I was exactly the opposite.

It was lab day in science. Mr. Fleming gave out instructions and set us loose to find partners. Normally I was partners with Franklin and probably still would have been this time, too, but before I could blink, I heard someone say,

"Sorry, Elise already asked me."

I turned to see Caroline talking to Amanda, who scowled and went to find someone else. Kate and Lindsay already seemed to be together. Ha, ha . . . Amanda, the odd girl out.

Caroline whispered, "Can we be lab partners?"

"Sure."

Franklin had heard the whole thing. He found a boy to be his partner.

I went with Caroline to collect our materials. The lab was about simple machines and work. We took a series of planks, wooden carts, springs, and pulleys out into the hallway to see what was best for moving the load, our science textbook, different distances.

"What was that about?" I asked.

"Amanda's my friend, but she thinks I'll do all the work."

"And you're still friends with her?"

"Hanging out and doing work together are different. Like last night I went to her house and it was really fun. She painted my nails—see, Pearlescent Pink—then when she said, 'Let's do the language arts homework,' I said I had to go home. Here, let's start with the horizontal distances. What do you think will be the best way?"

"Use the flat cart. We can make a ramp with the planks so the cart can run down and then speed along the distance."

Caroline set up the ramp. We ran the cart a couple times and used a stopwatch to time it. When I recorded the information, I noticed that my nails were broken off at different lengths. Amanda would probably have told me how gross they were.

"Do you think she's mean?"

"Amanda?"

"Yeah."

Caroline shrugged. "She's never been mean to me."

"She's mean to other people. Really mean."

Caroline picked up a cart, spun its wheels, and thought. "She was never like that before. It's like she wants to seem tougher now. I don't really know what's going on with her. I'll ask. Maybe she'll cut it out."

I didn't mention that Amanda's seeming "tough" included lunch-smashing, because I didn't want Caroline to pick Amanda over me if she knew this was a fight. Instead I spun the wheels on one of the other carts and asked, "What are you friends with her for, anyway?"

"We've always been friends, ever since kindergarten."

That sounded like me and Franklin. Sometimes you are friends with someone just because you're used to it, and maybe you forget why it happened in the first place.

I looked down the hallway to where Franklin was working. He seemed to be having fun. It really was his kind of project. Was he giving all the instructions? Did the other kid mind?

What were we fighting about, again?

Trying to figure out why things change is probably even harder than trying to figure out how they started.

When I got home, Annie and Ava were on the couch in the living room, nursing. I tried to hurry past, but Annie saw me.

"Sit for a minute, Elise."

I sat across from them, tapping my feet.

"Ava would like to get to know you," Annie said, "when she's not busy."

It felt like she wanted me to laugh, so I did, a little.

But I was thinking about the picture of Mom with the pregnant stomach. With me in it.

"Annie?"

"Hmm?"

"How much do you love Ava?"

"More than the moon and the stars and the sun combined. More than the whole world."

"When did you know?"

"When I first saw her." Annie changed Ava's position and looked back up at me.

"And you will love her always, no matter what?"

"Yes."

"Do you love her enough that, even if it meant you couldn't live another day, you would want her to live instead?"

"Yes."

"Even if she grew up to be a serial killer?"

"Are you saying I'm going to raise a serial killer?" Annie laughed.

"No, I'm just . . ." I looked down at my lap.

"Come here, Elise," Annie said. "Come sit with us." I moved to the couch. She shifted Ava to her shoulder. "Never, ever doubt how much a mother loves her child. Even before she is born."

With that, Ava spit up.

I headed to the kitchen for a snack. Aunt Bessie said, "Elise! I made cookies this morning. Maybe you could still smell them and that's why you came by?"

I smiled. "I just feel like hanging out."

"Good. Help yourself. I'm going to get dinner started. Pot roast needs to cook for a long time. Get your homework out and keep me company."

The cookies were still a little soft. Mmm, chocolate with melty butterscotch chips. I poured myself a glass of milk and dunked the cookies as I ate.

Aunt Bessie had gone back to chopping veggies at the counter. But she asked, "You want to talk about something?"

"No. I mean, yes. I . . . I think I want to visit Mom."

"We can do that," Aunt Bessie said. "It's probably been too long, hasn't it?"

I nodded.

"Do you want to plant some flowers? Like we used to?"

"I wanted to go alone," I said. "We'd have to go in the car to plant flowers."

"Not necessarily," she said. "There's just enough room on Hugh's bike for what you'd need."

I abandoned my cookies and we went out to the yard. Aunt Bessie dug up some mums, repotted them, and put them in the bicycle basket. She added a watering can—"There'll be somewhere to fill it"—and a trowel. "Ready?"

I straddled the bike, my feet barely touching the ground as I kept it steady.

Ready? "Well," I said, "here I go."

The cemetery is out along our school-bus route to town. Usually I pass it without even thinking about who's in there, because I'm so used to it. It took a long time to pedal there with the full basket.

At the cemetery, I set the bike against a tree. I walked through the headstones, and eventually I found them, Louisa Celeste and John Peter Bertrand, chiseled into one block. I stood, just looking.

I didn't know what to do with my hands. I put them in my jeans pockets, took them out, put them in my sweatshirt pockets, took them out.

Well, it wasn't like she was going to talk first.

I sat on my knees in the grass in front of the marble stone.

"Hi, uh, Mom," I started. "Dad—uh—I think Dad wanted me to get to know you. Well, a long time ago he did, but I'm here now. You have a pretty spot. . . ."

I tore up some of the dry grass in my fists. Then I realized it probably wasn't a very nice thing to do. I let the blades go and brushed my hands on my jeans.

"Is it my fault you're here?"

Cold stone never answered anyone.

"Well, it probably wasn't worth it. I'm bad at everything and nobody but our family likes me. I can't even keep one friend."

I wiped my nose on my sleeve.

"I'm really sorry."

I lay down on the grass, a little closer to them.

"I brought you something," I said when I eventually remembered. "I'll go get it."

I walked back to the bike and wheeled it over. I did my best digging two holes, one in front of each name. There was a little house nearby for the gardeners' supplies and I filled up the watering can at a spigot. After I had the flowers in place and watered, the plot looked a lot more cheerful.

Back home, Aunt Bessie met me on the porch and folded me into her arms. When she finally let go, she held out something. It looked like a necklace.

"It's the key. I took it out of the door where you left it. You can wear it, if you like."

"Thanks." I slipped it over my head. The key felt light, resting gently below my collarbone, near my heart.

Another Surprise

I didn't dream at all. That was nice. When I woke up, I felt rested. Uncle Hugh hadn't even knocked on the door yet to tell me it was time for school. I was thinking about Franklin. I felt so much better today, and maybe what had happened really wasn't his fault. We could try again.

As I lay in bed, I noticed something that could only mean one thing:

I *was* dreaming.

My daybed is pushed up against a window, so I can see the windowsill through the white-painted bars.

Sitting on the windowsill was a key.

I closed my eyes and opened them. Then I closed them again and counted to ten. The key was still there. I reached through the bars and picked it up.

It felt cool and smooth.

It had to be a key to another one of the barn rooms, didn't it?

Maybe it wasn't. Maybe I was just being hopeful.

The possibilities:

Dream: key won't open door to a barn room, because you're always left hanging in dreams.

Dream: key opens a barn room, but room is empty.

Dream: key opens a barn room, but room has something scary inside (like a dragon).

Real life: key isn't for the barn rooms.

Real life: key opens door to a barn room (inside, I find . . . ?).

In dreams, it doesn't usually matter where things come from. They can just appear for no reason. But in real life, things have to come from somewhere. Someone would have had to have put the key there. Uncle Hugh and Aunt Bessie were the most likely suspects. Had they had the keys all the time? But then why wouldn't they have given them to me before?

I could just ask them, but something made me hesitant. What if I *had* dreamed the key up, and they thought I was crazy?

I got dressed before I went to have breakfast so I could have more time to think. I slipped the key into the pocket of my jeans; that way, I'd know if it was still there and real, or, if it vaporized later, that would prove I'd imagined the whole thing.

Aunt Bessie had scrambled eggs waiting. She was already washing the frying pan at the sink.

"Did you put something in my room?" I asked as I carefully sprinkled salt and pepper over my eggs.

"Yes," she said. "Fourteen pairs of socks that I found left all over your room instead of in the hamper, washed, dried, balled up, and returned to you. They're on your desk.

I'm glad you noticed so you can put them away where they belong."

"Oh great, thanks," I said. I hadn't noticed the socks at all. But I figured the key wasn't from Aunt Bessie. She seemed all business. "Where's Uncle Hugh?"

"He left early for deliveries."

I updated my suspect list:

~~Aunt Bessie~~

Uncle Hugh. Was it a coincidence that he'd left early?

I didn't really have anyone else to add to my list.

Unless the key was coming from someone else entirely. What if Dad . . .

I shook the crazy thought out of my head.

"You need to get going," Aunt Bessie said. "It's a little later than usual. I let you sleep."

I gulped down my orange juice. I had to get to the barn, but I didn't want Aunt Bessie to notice, and I didn't think I could sneak off now. Especially since I had something else to sneak. I opened the fridge and slipped a cold bottle out. Aunt Bessie didn't turn around from the dishes.

I hurried to brush my teeth; grabbed my lunch, jacket, and backpack; and rushed out the door. On the way down the porch steps, I put my hand over my pocket. The key was still inside.

Franklin was waiting at the bus stop, standing with a few other kids. When I showed up, he looked at me. I motioned for him to come over.

"What?" he asked.

I pulled the bottle of cream soda out of my jacket. "Here."

"Thanks?" he said, with a question mark.

"Come over later?" I said, also with a question mark. "We have a puzzle to finish."

"Yeah, okay," Franklin said.

"Okay?"

"Yeah, okay."

Then he tried to take the metal cap off his soda with his bare hand, but he couldn't. I took the bottle, opened it, and handed it back.

He stood next to me and slurped quickly; you can't eat or drink on the bus and Franklin isn't a rule breaker. He's also not a litterbug, but he agreed to leave the bottle on the side of the road if I promised to help him remember to pick it up after school.

On the bus, I filled him in about what had been going on at home. How the key I'd found in the barn had opened that room. How probably all those rooms that had been locked up there forever were for me.

"Why didn't you tell me? You had a real-life mystery!" Franklin said. "*The Mystery in the Barn*. That would be the title."

"It's not done yet." I touched the key in my pocket. I didn't tell him I had it. I was still afraid it might disappear. Or that it wouldn't be a key to *The Mystery in the Barn* at all.

Maybe making up with Franklin so easily was part of the dream. Maybe I still hadn't woken up.

• • •

I knew I was awake when Amanda threw my lunch in the bottom of the locker, I reached my hand in to get it, and she slammed the locker shut, right on my fingernails.

I screamed, pulling my hand back. My fingers were bright red with white streaks under the nails, throbbing.

No way I could still be asleep.

This was my real life.

Franklin appeared as Amanda gave me a nasty grin and walked away.

"What's the matter?" he asked.

"My hand got shut in the door."

"You need ice," he said. "Otherwise, your fingers will get all swollen. You didn't hit your thumb, right?"

I imagined sitting in class next to Amanda with ice on my fingers. I had to act like she hadn't hurt me.

"No. I'll be fine."

In language arts, Mrs. Wakefield announced that she was going to do reading assessments. We would each have to sit for an oral quiz about our class reading (*The Call of the Wild*), talk about our independent reading, and set goals in a private conference. It would take two days to get through the whole class, so we had a long list of silent classwork to do.

Of course I couldn't start on the list of new assignments until after my conference, because I wasn't ready. I sat biting the nails on my good hand as I tried to scan the assigned chapters. I'd read them in patches. What if she asked detailed questions about something I hadn't bothered to read?

I glanced around. Two people got to work right away: Caroline and Franklin. Other people—like Amanda, Kate, and Lindsay—were whispering to each other.

Mrs. Wakefield was going alphabetically, so it wasn't long until my turn. I brought my book and sat across from her. I was glad that so many people were talking. No one would be able to hear my conference. Mrs. Wakefield was ready to take notes on a clipboard.

"Did you hurt your hand?"

"What? Oh, no. I mean, yeah . . . um, I was just being clumsy."

She gave me a funny look, but I didn't mention the locker trouble again. She'd never listened to it before. What would be different now?

"Well, when we're done you can get ice if you need to. This will be a lot like answering homework questions, but out loud. You should make a statement and back it up with specific details from the text. We've been talking a lot about theme. Can you define that term?"

"I think it's . . . ," I began, "a big idea in a story, but it's kind of . . . underneath."

"What do you mean by 'underneath'?"

"Kind of hidden. The author doesn't just say it. You have to think about it."

"Can you identify a theme in *The Call of the Wild?*"

"Courage."

"Can you support that with details?"

I opened my copy of the book and started flipping through it. The student who'd used it before me had highlighted things. Maybe they would help me.

"I don't know." I couldn't pretend to be a confident student for that long. Maybe Mrs. Wakefield would feel sorry for me if I acted like I had trouble. "I'm not so good on the spot. I need a while to think about things."

"Could you talk about it a little? To help you get started? It might get easier as you go along."

I shook my head.

"Then why don't you choose an aspect of the book to talk about? Is there something in particular that you like or dislike about the book?"

"I like the survival stuff."

She was probably looking for something deeper. I was bombing.

"Would you say that the work has a theme of survival?"

"Sure."

Mrs. Wakefield wrote some notes.

"Let's move on to your independent reading. You have to hand in your reading journal with ten books logged by Thanksgiving. Are you about halfway?"

I thought about my reading journal: empty. I nodded that yes, I was about halfway.

"What are you reading now?" she asked.

"I'm between books."

"So what did you just finish?"

"*The Secret Garden*," I lied. I looked down at my fingernails, which were turning a bit purple.

"Can you tell me about it?"

Luckily, I'd seen the movie.

"Yeah. This girl finds a key that opens a garden that's been locked for like ten years. . . ." I trailed off, suddenly lost in my own thoughts. My hand felt my pocket. The key was still there, even though I was sure I was awake now. I shivered.

"Would you say that book was too easy, too difficult, or just right for you? . . . Elise?"

"What? Oh. Uh . . . it was fine."

"What do you think you will read next?"

"I'm not sure."

"This is for you." Mrs. Wakefield handed me a printout. "Some book suggestions that are probably on target for you. I'd like at least five of your reading reports in your journal to be on them, okay? Make sure you're keeping up with your reading."

"Thanks," I said, taking the list, folding it into quarters, and sticking it inside my copy of *The Call of the Wild*. Like I'd look at *that* again.

Finally (finally, finally, finally), the day ended. Franklin picked up the bottle we'd left by the side of the road.

"Come by later to work on the puzzle?" I asked.

He nodded and headed home.

I didn't want him to come over right away, because I needed to try to unlock the next room, by myself.

Uncle Hugh's truck wasn't in the driveway. I dropped my stuff on the front porch and went out to the barn.

I reminded myself that maybe the key wouldn't go to any of the rooms. But the third lock I tried—a room on the end—turned with a satisfying *click*.

This room was much bigger, a true room rather than a closet. It was wall-to-wall, floor-to-ceiling filled with books. There was an old-fashioned wooden desk and chair. I walked over to the desk and found another note on top. This one said, SEEK TO LEARN.

"What is this?" I asked out loud. "National Get-Elise-to-Read Day?"

I left the key in the lock and went downstairs.

Books

"Your dad collected quite a library. He must have stored it up there," Uncle Hugh explained at dinner. "He loved books. Your mom, too. Where did the key come from?"

"It just showed up in my room."

Uncle Hugh looked at Aunt Bessie, who shrugged. He went back to stirring the salmon-cream-sauce noodles on his plate. If one of them was leaving the keys, the other didn't seem to know about it.

"Did Dad spend a lot of time reading?" I asked.

"He always had a book, wherever he went."

"That was nice, later, when he was sick. He didn't have to give up his favorite thing," Aunt Bessie added.

"And Mom?"

"She was more of a sit-in-her-pink-chair than a read-on-the-go kind of girl."

"What did they like to read?"

"Hmm . . . Lots of things, I'd guess. I didn't ask much. Walking up to someone and saying 'Whatchya readin'?' is obnoxious."

"No one's ever asked me that," I said.

"You're not often caught reading."

"So . . . why would Dad leave me a library?"

"Maybe it was something special to him that he could give you," Annie chimed in.

"But why would he lock it up?" I asked. "Why couldn't the library just have been open all those years?"

"What's a three-year-old going to do with all those books?" Uncle Hugh pointed out. "Color in them? Maybe he wanted you to be old enough to appreciate them. It's not like we don't have plenty of books already."

"Can I finish my homework out there? There's a big desk."

"That's okay with me," Aunt Bessie said.

"We'll stop by to visit," Uncle Hugh said.

"Okay." Double okay: the barn could be creepy in the dark.

Uncle Hugh walked up with me, carrying a standing lamp. I had my backpack and all my work, which I spread out on the old desk.

"It's nice to know that I'll never run out of things to read," Uncle Hugh said. He started looking through the shelves, and suddenly he was laughing!

"What?" I asked.

He picked up a battered paperback. "Your dad's joke book. He used to carry this around *all* the time, when he was about ten. Could never get him to stop telling them."

He handed it to me. It felt very worn, but I liked it. I flipped through, found a whole page of "Why did the chicken cross the road?" Dad had even written in some of his own: "Because on the other side it was Thanksgiving, so only turkeys had to worry." I wasn't sure if that was funny, but it made me smile anyway.

"I've been looking for this one." Uncle Hugh slid a thin book off the shelf. "The town library didn't have it. Can I borrow it?"

"Sure. Take whatever you want."

Uncle Hugh had already put on his glasses, reading as he walked out.

I opened all the desk drawers. There were some old ball-point pens, a couple paper clips, and a yellow lined notepad. Plenty of room for my own things, if I wanted. If I liked working in the library.

It felt very good and official to open my science book flat on the desk and flip through the pages while I answered the questions using the Caroline Method. After I finished but before I started math, I looked at Dad's books.

All the books were for grown-ups. There was no sense to how they were arranged—not by topic or author. Maybe it made sense to Dad.

"What's up?" a voice asked.

I jumped about a mile. Then I realized it was just Franklin. "Jerk. You don't just sneak up on somebody."

"Sorry. How'd you get in here?"

"I should ask you the same question."

"Annie told me you were out here. So—you opened another room."

I told him how the key had appeared.

"There are so many books in here!"

"Like a thousand," I agreed.

"More like three thousand."

"Three thousand?"

"Well, twenty bookcases, each with about six shelves." He pointed. "Twenty-four books on this shelf, which rounds to about twenty-five books on each. So there are about three thousand books in this room."

We stared around at the bookshelves.

"Feel like reading?" I asked.

"I feel like having hot cocoa. And doing the space puzzle."

"Yeah." I followed him, leaving my homework. The puzzle seemed more important.

Caroline was sitting with her usual group at lunch when I spotted her the next day, but the others left eventually. She started reading in the middle of the noisy lunchroom. She really could fall into her own world.

When Franklin finished eating and left to check on the mold he was growing for extra credit in science, I went to sit with Caroline.

She looked up from her book without marking the place. I remembered what Aunt Bessie had said about it being annoying to ask someone what she's reading, so I skipped that question.

"Would you be interested in a room full of books?" Maybe that was an odd thing to ask.

"I guess so," Caroline said. "Where is it?"

"In my barn."

"You have a room full of books in your barn?"

"Well, I do now. I mean, it's been there, I just didn't know about it."

"You didn't?"

I filled her in on the details. I have to admit, they sounded pretty crazy. But she was curious about the rooms and keys.

She was busy that afternoon, but the next day she got a pass to come home with me on the bus.

Which really seemed to annoy Franklin. When we got off the bus, he headed toward his own house.

"This is a *lot* of books." Caroline walked into the room and turned slowly. "Lucky! You have your own library!"

"That's one way to look at it. It was my dad's. All the books are for grown-ups."

Caroline walked over to a shelf and picked up a book. She opened it and smelled the pages. When I gave her a funny look, she said, "Books smell really good."

"You can borrow some."

Caroline ran her fingers along the spines. She seemed to judge books as much by their covers as by the way they smelled and the way the paper felt under her fingertips.

"They're not all grown-up books," she said.

"I think they are."

"Nope." She pulled one off a shelf. "*Winnie-the-Pooh*. They're just disguised. Hardcovers without jackets."

She handed me *Winnie-the-Pooh*. I opened it, flipped through.

"Someone read this to me," I said. "I think a teacher."

I sniffed the book like Caroline had. I closed my eyes.

It wasn't a teacher. It was a man's voice reading. And I wasn't sitting in a desk or a circle of other kids . . . I was in bed, with pillows and Bunny-Rabbit and a sleepy feeling. The memory was so shadowy I could hardly catch it.

"Dad read this to me."

"Well, here, this whole section has kids' books."

I pulled several books from their places. Then I heard the smallest noise of metal moving.

When I looked at the shelf, there was a key!

"Caroline, look!" I said. "Another key! Just here on the shelf!"

She took it from me. "It's dusty. I bet it's been here the whole time."

The dust on the shelf showed the outline of a key. The key probably *had* been locked in this room the whole time, in plain sight on the shelf.

"Come on!" I said.

I ran into the hallway with Caroline behind me. I jammed the key into doorknobs until it fit. When I pushed the door open . . .

An empty room. Not even a note!

I stood there, panting. Caroline peered over my shoulder, just as confused.

"Why would he lock an empty room?" I asked eventually.

"Another mystery."

"More like a dead end." We were both quiet for a long time.

"Maybe I should go," Caroline said gently.

"No, stay. You haven't picked out any books yet. Are you hungry? We're having sloppy joes tonight. Come on."

Caroline followed me outside. "You have so many leaves! I used to love to go to Amanda's and make a big leaf pile. We'd jump in it for hours. She doesn't like to do that anymore."

"Don't you have your own trees?"

Caroline shook her head. "We don't even have a yard. We live above the deli in town."

"We could play in the leaves."

"Really?"

"Yeah. Hang on." I slipped back into the barn and got two rakes.

"Here." Caroline ran and stood under a tree near the driveway with branches that hung low around our shoulders. "We can make the pile here and then jump out of the tree."

We scrambled around trying to make the leaf pile as quickly as possible. Caroline made neat sweeps with the rake, but every time I looked over at her, she swung her rake fast and threw the leaves up high in the air with a goofy smile. It made me think of a clown doing something in a hurry. I couldn't help laughing.

It took a long time, maybe an hour, to get the pile deep enough for us. We were both sweating even though it was getting kind of cold out. The sun had almost set.

"You first," I said. "It was your idea."

"Okay." Caroline climbed onto the lowest branch and flopped backward into the pile. "Ah! That was great! But, ouch . . ."—she stood up and rubbed her bum—"my tailbone."

I had never before seen anyone play in leaves in tights and a skirt. She didn't seem to mind, though.

I climbed onto the low branch. I wouldn't hurt my tailbone.

"Belly flop!" I yelled, spreading my arms and heading front-first into the leaves.

"Ha, ha! Good idea!" Caroline scooted back into the tree and echoed my battle cry, not giving me even a second to get out of the way. She landed on top of me and we both howled, laughing so hard.

"Get up!" I threw a fistful of leaves at her.

"Oh yeah?" She scooped up a handful of leaves and rubbed them against my head. We gave each other noogies until Caroline tumbled back and spread her arms to make leaf angels.

Car lights bounced down the driveway.

"Who's that?" Caroline sat up.

"Uncle Hugh."

"Come on, let's hide and surprise him."

We scrambled under the leaves, completely hidden.

"Wait, wait," I whispered. The car stopped. Uncle Hugh's feet crunched the gravel, his door slammed. "Now."

"*Boooo!*" We both jumped up and threw as many leaves as we could.

Uncle Hugh wasn't scared. He started laughing! Then he wiped the tears out of his eyes. "Cricket, who's this crazy kid?"

"Caroline," I said.

"Wonderful. Welcome, Caroline." He turned to go in. "Come on. You'll have some cleaning up to do. Aunt Bessie won't let two hoodlums come to her dinner table." I looked at Caroline: her usually smooth hair was all fuzzy and full of broken bits of leaves. Her skirt was pulled up and twisted and there were leaves stuck all over her clothes, too. I probably looked just as bad.

We picked up our backpacks and ran to the porch. We tried to get off all the leaves; the ones on our clothes were easy. But there were also leaves *in* our shirts. We had another fit of laughing when Caroline found some clumped inside her tights.

"Girls!" Uncle Hugh called from inside.

"Coming!"

When we paraded into the kitchen, Aunt Bessie said, "There's a hairbrush in the bathroom."

We giggled some more on our way there. I handed Caroline my hairbrush and she easily brushed her hair out. Mine would be a lot harder: my hair tie had disappeared while we were having noogie fights.

"Here, let me." Caroline kept the brush. I sat on the edge of the tub and she combed my hair carefully, starting at the bottom. After she'd gotten out all the leaves, she put my hair in two braids. "Even if my hair were long, I couldn't have braids. My hair is so slippery they don't stay in."

I stood and admired the braids in the mirror. "You want dinner?"

"Okay," Caroline said. "I'll call my mom." She got permission to stay.

"Now that you two are cleaned up," Aunt Bessie said when we arrived back in the kitchen, "you're in charge of the sauce."

She found an extra apron for Caroline. The sauce splattered everywhere, but that was part of the fun.

"Who's this?" Caroline asked when Annie brought Ava to her high chair.

"Ava. Ava, meet . . ."

"Caroline," Caroline and I answered together.

"Hi, Caroline. I'm Annie. Want to feed her? I think it's peas and plums tonight." Annie got the containers of baby food.

"Sure!" Caroline said. She talked and sang to Ava while she fed her, and she did a good job. She even used the bib to wipe up Ava's dribbles. I'd have thought they were too yucky to touch.

Uncle Hugh came in.

"You like babies?" he asked Caroline.

"Yeah. I have two little sisters. They aren't babies anymore, but I used to help when they were."

At dinner, Caroline answered all of Uncle Hugh's questions and laughed at his jokes and passed the salad and got sloppy-joe sauce on her cheeks, which she neatly wiped away with her napkin without being embarrassed. And she helped me tell everyone about finding the next key and how the room turned out to be empty.

"Maybe there just wasn't time to fill it," Annie suggested.

"Nah," Uncle Hugh said. "The way John liked puzzles . . . if he locked an empty room, there's a reason."

Invisible Things

Amanda was mad that I was hanging out with Caroline. She was squashing my lunch worse than ever. One morning it was under *everything* in the locker.

And she tried to slam the locker door on my hand. Again. But I got my hand out of the way just in time. She looked at me and said, "Oops."

I overheard her talking to Caroline and she said, "It's not like I'm the one hanging out with *losers*." I couldn't hear what Caroline said back.

Did Caroline think Franklin and I were losers? She still sat with Amanda at lunch, which was what she usually did, so maybe it meant nothing. But in the hallway she asked me what Franklin and I were doing after school. We were heading to Leonard's and then out for burgers. I told her she could come, if she wanted to.

At the hardware store, Franklin took Caroline to meet everyone and I went to see Leonard.

"Hey, Leonard," I said.

"Where have you been? You *are* too busy to visit old Leonard."

"No. Ta-da! I'm here."

"Yeah, well, long time no see." Leonard didn't look up at me as he counted all the twenties in the drawer, then the tens.

"You mad?"

"Nah. It's just a sign you're growing up, is all. I'm feeling like an old man."

"You aren't!" I said. "You're nowhere near as old as Uncle Hugh."

He laughed and shut the drawer. "Who's your new friend?"

"Caroline."

"That's nice. It's nice to see you with a friend who's a girl. You'll probably be needing some of those."

"What's wrong with Franklin?"

"Nothing's wrong with Franklin." Leonard looked me up and down. "What's that book you're carrying around?"

"Just something of Dad's," I said, pulling *The Little Prince* out from under my arm. I'd found it in the library. It was the pictures that caught me.

"Really?" Leonard asked.

"Yeah, he left me a whole bunch of books. I don't know if you've ever been upstairs in the barn, but there's all these locked rooms up there. Turns out they're for me, from Dad. So far I've opened three of them."

"What'd you find?"

"Some things of Mom's, a room full of Dad's books, and then the third room was just empty."

"Totally empty?"

"Yep. Why would Dad lock an empty room?"

Leonard shook his head. "Knowing him, there was a reason."

"That's what Uncle Hugh said. Do you know the reason?"

"Nope. But I don't think I'm supposed to know. I think *you're* supposed to know."

"Well, I don't."

"Can you put down the book for a few minutes? How about you and your friends sweep up the floors for me, and then I'll give you a little cash and you can go get some burgers and milk shakes?"

I smiled. "That was the plan."

"Good."

Caroline and I dipped fries in our milk shakes. Then we swapped glasses, because she had vanilla and I had chocolate.

Milk-shake sharing left Franklin out. He tried his fries in his soda.

"How is it?" Caroline asked.

Franklin made a face.

He poured a pool of ketchup into the cardboard condiment holder. When he ate, he got smudges of ketchup on his face.

I tossed Franklin napkins from the metal dispenser on the table. He wiped his face but just ended up spreading the ketchup around more.

"Nice work, gross-out," I told him.

Franklin set the napkins aside. I threw a French fry at him. He used his sleeve to rub his face where the fry hit him, and his sleeve got streaked with red ketchup. Not a whole lot neater.

Caroline didn't seem bothered by Franklin at all. She reached over with a fry to share the ketchup.

"What would happen if you had a milk shake?" Caroline asked.

"A bad rash," Franklin answered. "And severe diarrhea."

I couldn't *believe* that Franklin would talk about diarrhea when we were eating with Caroline.

Caroline said, "It might be worth it. Once in a while."

Franklin shook his head so quickly that Caroline and I couldn't help laughing.

That night I couldn't sleep, so I got up to get a drink of water and walk around. Aunt Bessie and Uncle Hugh had gone to bed. Annie was asleep on the couch. In Annie and Ava's room, Ava was awake making pouty noises. I wasn't sure what to do, but I didn't want to wake Annie up if she was so tired that she fell asleep on the couch. I could at least *try* to see what was wrong with Ava.

"Hey," I whispered softly. "Hey there, it's okay."

As I peeked into the crib, I saw Ava's bottom lip curled down, shiny with spit, ready to let out a real cry.

"I really can't feed you," I said. "But I can pat you a little."

I rubbed Ava's small pink-pajamaed tummy. "There, does that feel good?" She looked at me expectantly.

"I'll be right back," I said. I tiptoed to my room, picked up my book, and returned to Ava.

Babies like the sound of people reading, right?

I put on the small lamp and sat down in the beautiful blue rocking chair and began to read. The book felt different, out loud in the middle of the night. I tried to keep my voice quiet, but steady. I paused at several lines, feeling them.

"Ava? What if the third room isn't empty, but full of invisible things?"

I closed my eyes and pictured the bare space. I tried to picture it with my heart. But I didn't see anything. It was still just an empty room.

Knowing

Pizza night.

Once a month, Uncle Hugh and Aunt Bessie go out on a date to a restaurant. Franklin comes over to hang out with me and we get a whole cheese pizza just for us.

I didn't bother to get a plate. I smashed two pieces together for my pizza sandwich and bit down on the point. The gush of steaming sauce smothered my tongue. *Mmm.*

Franklin took one piece, put it on a plate, and started picking off the cheese.

I tossed my crusts onto Franklin's rejected cheese pile and got my next pair of pieces.

Franklin wasn't talking much.

"What's the matter with you?" I asked.

"Nothing." He got up from the table and poured a glass of orange soda. He didn't ask if I wanted one.

After dinner, we worked on the puzzle. Franklin silently connected pieces. Now that the spaceship and Earth were put together, there was a lot of boring night sky to do.

A puzzle-piece fight would be more fun. I threw one at Franklin's forehead to get things started.

"Hey!" he cried, too loudly. It couldn't have hurt.

"What's wrong with you?"

"Nothing."

"Liar."

Franklin seemed to stew for a minute, and then asked, "Why did you invite me over?"

"It's pizza night. You always come over on pizza night."

"Why didn't you invite Caroline?"

"Caroline?"

"Yeah, she's always around now."

"She's not. She doesn't even eat lunch with us."

"Well, you two seem to get along great and I don't trust her."

"Why not?"

"She's friends with the enemy."

"What?"

"Yeah, the enemy: Amanda. She's so mean to you."

"Caroline's nice."

"How do you know?"

"Because she acts nice."

"Exactly. It could be an *act*." Franklin always gave people the benefit of the doubt. What was his problem? "You don't really know her."

"It feels more like I don't know *you*. You aren't acting like you." The Franklin I knew liked everybody. Even Diana the cat girl. The Franklin I knew had never been mad at me for making a new friend.

But actually, I had never really made a new friend before. It had always been just me and Franklin.

I ran out of things to say, right in the middle of our conversation. I took half of the white-speckled black pieces from Franklin and examined the stars, as if I could learn them by heart.

"All by yourself today, Cricket?" Leonard asked.

I nodded.

"Finish that book?"

"Yeah. I read it a couple times. And picked out some new ones."

I'd stacked them on the desk in the library. I was doing my homework in there almost every night now, and having a lot less trouble getting it done. At least if I forgot to put the homework back in my bag, I knew where it would be. Most nights, Uncle Hugh worked quietly downstairs in his workshop, so I wasn't out there by myself.

"You starting to like reading a little more?" Leonard asked.

"Maybe." I had even filled out a couple entries in my reading journal for Mrs. Wakefield.

"Maybe's a start," he said. "Interested in earning some snack money?"

"Sure. Aunt Bessie's not coming to get me until five."

"Everything okay with your friends?"

"Yeah." I hadn't invited either of them. Franklin had sat through lunch like his soy milk was sour, even though Caroline wasn't with us. And Caroline seemed to be included in Amanda's afternoon plans.

Leonard gave me one of my favorite jobs, mixing the trial-sized-can paint samples that people requested. I liked knowing that even though there are hundreds of colors to pick from on the little sample cards, they're all just a couple bases with extra color squirts to change them. I got paint on my hands and jeans. But everyone, even Aunt Bessie, knows that jeans look cooler with paint splotches.

At the burger place I got fries covered in cheese—a treat I never order with Franklin—and a vanilla milk shake. It felt good just to sit there on my own. It was a little lonely—there were other tables of older kids from school—but really, it was okay.

The next day I didn't ask anyone to hang out, either, and went right home after school. I visited Aunt Bessie in the kitchen and made myself a peanut-butter dipping plate of sliced apples, carrots, and celery. Then I went out to the library, threw my bag on the floor, and set the snack on the desk. I flopped into the chair, crunching a carrot, and something on the desk caught my eye. . . .

A key.

It hadn't been there yesterday.

Uncle Hugh was out on deliveries. I thought of asking Aunt Bessie if anyone had been out here today, get right down to sleuthing.

But that idea didn't feel right. It seemed like whoever was leaving the keys didn't want me to know who he or she was. I left that mystery for later and picked up the key.

∙ ∙ ∙

Taped to the wall was a message: CHOOSE TO LIVE,
CHOOSE TO LOVE.

There were pictures on the wall in this room, too.

In one, a man holds a newborn baby. The man is crying, but, underneath that, he has an expression of wonder.
He's in other pictures, smiling and looking happy as he plays
with a growing baby and toddler—on park swings . . . at the
beach . . . with blocks. In one picture, the toddler has become
a little girl. Her dark hair is just starting to grow beyond her
shoulders. The man stands behind her, brushing it, but his
eyes seem sad and faraway. In the last picture, he looks old.
His hair is only wisps, his skin pale. He sits in a wheelchair.
The girl in his lap holds a book, laughing.

This room was about Dad and me. Together.

The only other thing in the room was a sketchbook, its
pages full and puffy. It was just sitting, dusty, in the middle
of the floor. Aunt Bessie probably would have had a heart at-
tack, but I sat right down in the grime and opened the book.

It wasn't filled with sketches, but with words.

I started on the first page:

> . . . This morning we went to your favorite
> playground. It took us a long time to get
> there because your pink sneakers were
> missing. Finally, Hugh found one under the
> couch (with sixteen dusty blocks, seven
> Cheerios, and one AWOL stuffed rabbit), and

you discovered the other in your toy chest. How can your shoes get lost every day?

By the time we got to the park, all the swings were taken, but you headed to the sandbox instead. Then you wanted to climb on the monkey bars, which are too high for you to reach. I helped you up there and you moved your arms from bar to bar, pretending you were moving on your own. . . .

. . . Today it was raining, so we didn't even have to look for your sandy shoes. You sat with your face pressed to the window, waiting for the rain to stop.

Eventually, I got you into the kitchen for a "cooking" project. We made peanut-butter toast. There was peanut butter everywhere! You put on all kinds of toppings—Cheerios, marshmallows, chocolate chips. . . . You were one big sticky mess when you were done eating! It was straight to the bath after that. . . .

. . . Today was your first trip to get a haircut. I didn't even want to cut your hair, but Bessie told me it would grow out nicer if we got it cut along the way.

They made a big fuss over you at the barbershop. My barber put a board across the arms of one of the chairs for you to sit on. He wrapped an old button-up shirt around you and set to work. You kept your eyes fixed on me watching you the whole time. Only when the haircut was done and I carried you over to the mirror did you look. "Pretty!" you announced. . . .

. . . I spent most of my day in the hospital for treatment, but Bessie tells me that you had a good day. You picked up colored leaves outside and brought them in and taped them in a notebook to keep.

I hate days when I don't see you. They happen more and more. . . .

. . . Today I came home after you were sleeping, and I sat by your bed for a little while, petting your hair, careful not to wake you from your dreams.

You looked a little bigger. You were growing, after all, even in the couple of days I was gone. And you will keep growing. You will change without me.

But I remind myself that I know you. I know your heart, and that will stay the same, so I will always know you. . . .

I had to put the book down after that one. It can be hard to read with water in your eyes.

He said he knew me, he knew me . . . but I was so little. Was it really true that inside, my heart was the same? From the sound of it, I wasn't even Cricket yet. And what did the note mean? CHOOSE TO LIVE, CHOOSE TO LOVE?

I shut the journal, even though I had only read some of it, and went downstairs. Uncle Hugh wasn't back yet, so I headed inside the house.

The door to Annie and Ava's room was open. I could hear Ava, cooing, waking up from her nap. Annie didn't seem to be around, so I walked over to the crib. Ava was tasting her foot and talking to it.

"Hi, Ava," I whispered. I reached out to stroke her cheek. It was soft and a little wet from being bumped by her spitty foot.

"Go ahead. Take her out." Annie had walked up behind me.

"I don't know how."

"Course you do. It's natural. Put your hands around her there, under her arms, and lift."

I put my hands around Ava where Annie had said to. I would have laughed or gotten mad if someone squeezed my middle like that, but Ava was used to being picked up. I lifted her out, making sure her toes cleared the bars. I held her stiffly, far from me.

Annie took my hands and helped them hold Ava under her butt and on her back, pressing her against me. It felt good, her little warm body, like a hug in which I did all the hugging.

"Now bring her over here so I can change that pee-pee diaper."

I followed Annie to the changing table, and she helped me lay Ava on the thick pad.

"She likes this, see?" Annie played "This Little Piggy" on Ava's toes, kissing them and blowing raspberries on the bottom of her feet. Ava shrieked and laughed.

My mother had never done that to me. Maybe Dad had?

"How did you find out she liked that?" I asked.

"I don't know. It was just a game we started to play. Wasn't it, sweetie?" she asked Ava in a soft voice. Ava smiled back. "There, all done." Annie sat Ava up.

"Grab some of her toys. We'll go to the living room."

In the living room she laid Ava down on a blanket on the floor.

"Will you stay with her while I get some laundry started?" I must have looked nervous. "You don't have to do anything, just stay here."

She left. Ava looked around.

"Hi," I said. "It's okay." I picked up one of the toys, a fat bumblebee with crinkly wings. "See? It's okay." I turned the bee a little in front of her, making the wings crackle. I moved it closer to her. She looked a little cross-eyed, trying to focus, but when I touched it to her nose and said, "Bop!" she laughed. I pulled the bee back out. "Buzz . . . bop!" Ava laughed again. I put the bee down and placed my hand near hers. She wrapped her fist around my pinky. I let her hold on.

Maybe Dad did know me as a little kid. Some things seemed the same—me losing things, loving peanut butter.

But I didn't lose things as much anymore. Other sides of me seemed to have come and gone—like me being a chirping cricket. Maybe now I was more like the Elise Dad knew than I'd been other times.

Kind of like how I really thought I knew Franklin and then he turned into a weirdo about Caroline. Where did that come from? Would he change back?

How could you ever really know someone, if they could change on you?

What did Dad mean by CHOOSE TO LOVE? What did choosing have to do with anything? Don't you either happen to love someone or not?

I looked down at Ava, who was looking up expectantly.

"Sorry." I picked up the stuffed bee again.

Uncle Hugh came home and found me with Ava. "Having fun?"

I shrugged. "Annie's doing laundry."

"Here," he said, lifting Ava off the floor and sitting down on the couch, settling her in his lap facing him. He made lovey-dovey faces and she responded with happy coos.

"Uncle Hugh?"

"Yes, Cricket?" He made a different face at Ava.

"I found a new key and room. It's about me and Dad together . . . but his note says 'Choose to live, choose to love.' What does that mean?"

Uncle Hugh looked at me then. "I'm going to tell you the truth, is that okay?"

"Yes."

"Good. What I think it means is this . . . when your mom died, your dad was so sad, he could have just become wrapped up in being sad, but he didn't; he chose to be a father to you. And when he got sick, he could have become wrapped up in being sick, but he chose to be a father to you. He chose to keep living, and he kept finding ways to show his love for you, no matter how hard things were."

While I thought about that, Uncle Hugh started asking Ava, "Do you have a wet diaper?" even though her mother had just changed it. She was laughing.

"What is he saying to me, though? Nothing like that is happening to me."

"Maybe not. But in life people come and go. We don't always have control over it. But we can control how we respond. We can keep going, keep living the best we can. We can love the people we have instead of shutting them out. We can do our best to get to know them in the time we have."

He turned back to Ava. "Like you, little one. How lucky we are to have you here with us. How lucky!"

"Where's Ava's dad?"

"He, unlike your dad, was just not interested."

"Just not interested?"

"Stated plainly, yes. He told Annie he didn't want to have children and left."

I looked at little Ava. She was just a baby. She didn't even know. She was still smiling and playing.

We can do our best to get to know them. . . .

Franklin was right that I didn't know Caroline too well—

but I knew enough to trust her—it was that slug Amanda I didn't know, except that as far as I *did* know, she was entirely awful.

Kind of like Uncle Hugh was saying, she was a person in my life. Wouldn't it make sense to give it a shot, see what made her tick?

Besides, would Caroline really be friends with someone who was only awful?

Spying on the Enemy

I paid attention to what Amanda did the next day.

She squashed my lunch (not a surprise).

She never waited for anyone; people caught up with her. Sometimes, Kate and Lindsay looked panicky when they thought she was heading off without them. That was funny.

She didn't raise her hand in any class we had together, but she did reply when Mr. Fleming asked her a question. She said, "What makes you think I would know?" What a stellar, polite student. Just what every teacher must dream of. He made her go to the principal's.

When we had a quiz in language arts, she went to the bathroom and skipped it. Mrs. Wakefield accepted her blank paper into the pile, but I bet she'd give it a zero—I'd watch when we got them back.

In gym, we played volleyball. She wouldn't even touch the ball when it came to her. The sporty girls looked annoyed, but no one said anything.

And it wasn't just me and Franklin she called names. I counted at least five other people. Not one did anything back to her.

She seemed completely rotten, but in control. She had started that control on day one by showing that she could be mean to people. No one had the courage to stand up to her, so she could have anything she wanted. She held everyone else in place, beneath her. I was pretty sure that Amanda didn't have any more to her than I already knew.

Franklin, determined to hate Amanda, didn't exactly understand what I wanted to learn, but was willing to help. "The problem is," he whispered to me when we were partners in social studies last period, "that you already know what she's like at school. If you really wanted to learn something about her, you'd have to be with her somewhere else."

I nodded. I'd have to do some better sleuthing.

The next day Caroline picked me to be her draft-editing partner in language arts. We had to swap rough drafts, read them, and give each other suggestions.

Caroline likes to get her work done, so I made sure we finished before I started a conversation. I also made sure that Amanda couldn't hear us.

"What's going on after school today?" I asked.

"Do you want to hang out?"

"No, I was just wondering what was up. Are . . . you know . . . people doing anything?"

"What people?"

"You know, Amanda, Kate, Lindsay . . ."

"Not today. Amanda gets picked up by her brother a couple days a week and no one hangs out on those days."

"I didn't know she had a brother. I've never seen her get picked up."

"She has him meet her on the other side of the soccer field at the lower parking lot."

I knew the place. A grove of trees and a couple rocks that kids used as benches.

"So what are you doing after school?" Caroline asked me.

"Just getting picked up."

It wasn't really a lie; if I stayed to spy on Amanda, I'd eventually have to call home to get a ride.

After last period, I told Franklin I wasn't going home on the bus. At our locker, Amanda quickly got her things and slammed the door.

"See ya, Scabular."

I opened the locker and grabbed a couple of books, hoping they were the right ones, and crammed them into my backpack. Then I scooted after her, careful to stay a good distance behind as she left the building.

The soccer field was more challenging because it was a big open space. I decided not to follow Amanda and ran along the school grounds in the other direction instead. I lost sight of her, but when I came out at the lower parking lot, she was waiting there. I stayed hidden in the trees.

It felt mean, spying. But what I wanted to know wasn't

bad. I was looking for another side of her. Maybe if I saw a side of her that was nice, things would be different at school. Maybe she wouldn't be so hateable.

Amanda sat on a rock bench, tugging her jean skirt down so her legs wouldn't touch the cold stone. Her jacket didn't seem warm enough, because she waited with her arms crossed tightly across her chest. Maybe her feet were cold, too, because she was tapping them even though no one was around to admire her shoes.

Eventually a car full of teenage boys pulled up. Amanda stood, straightened her skirt, and adjusted her backpack on her shoulders.

"Hurry up!" the driver called. Her brother. He had hair in his eyes and a sleepy expression. Jake and Alec looked a lot nicer than he did.

One of the boys in the back was hanging out the window smoking a cigarette. As Amanda approached, he blew smoke at her. "Want one?"

"No," Amanda said. It sounded like she was trying to make the "no" strong, like she was a little afraid of him.

"Your sister's an infant," the boy called to the driver.

"She won't tell on you, don't worry," Amanda's brother said back. "She's a—"

He called her something that I knew I wouldn't be repeating in front of Aunt Bessie, or even Franklin, for that matter. As the boy in the back slid over to make room for Amanda, he called her something even worse.

Amanda looked small. She slammed the car door and her brother started to drive away.

I felt a sinking in my stomach. I didn't know if Amanda had a nice side or not, but she definitely had a scared side. She had to be with people who treated her badly. I knew what that felt like, thanks to her.

Then my stomach dropped another full roller-coaster-ride level: as the car drove away, Amanda saw me, hiding behind a tree and watching her. Her mouth fell open, but closed quickly into a smirk as she narrowed her eyes at me.

She was saying, *You're dead meat. Big-time.*

"Do you have any . . . enemies?" I asked Leonard.

"Well, let's see," he said thoughtfully, stroking his chin. "Rehl's Hardware, across town. Does that count?"

"I don't know," I answered. "Does Rehl's Hardware bother you every day you come to work? And make it so you're afraid to come in? And so that you can't fall asleep at night just thinking about the morning?"

He thought some more. "Just a couple weeks ago, a guy came in with a receipt for a hammer he'd bought here and a sales ad for the same hammer at Rehl's, and he wanted to know why my hammer cost forty-nine cents more and could he have his forty-nine cents back?"

"Did you give it to him?"

"Yep."

"And that's the worst of it?"

"Pretty much. There's enough people in this town for two hardware stores, so I stay in business, Rehl's stays in business . . . things seem okay."

I was quiet, sitting on the counter. What would Amanda do to me tomorrow?

"What's the matter, Cricket?" Leonard asked. "Have you made an enemy?"

"No." I hadn't done anything wrong, so I hadn't made her my enemy. She'd picked me out. But this afternoon I'd made things one hundred times worse. Even though I'd seen her a little scared, I was even more scared of her. I was terrified.

In the morning, on the bus, Franklin said, "Lise? Lise? Lise?"

"What?" I jumped.

"What's the matter?"

"I . . . I couldn't do my math homework last night. I forgot my math book."

Franklin nodded. He took out his own math book, a binder, and a sheet of paper. He fished a pencil out of his constellations pencil case.

"Here." He handed everything to me.

I could have hugged him. But instead, I whispered what was really wrong: "Amanda's going to kill me."

"Don't worry," he said. "She can't really. It's against the law."

Franklin is too literal sometimes. There were loads of other ways your life could end in middle school.

• • •

Amanda was at our locker. I said, "Good morning."

"Good morning, buttwipe." She slammed the door and left.

I hesitated before putting my lunch up on the locker shelf. She hadn't hung around to smash it.

The morning went okay. Thanks to Franklin, I didn't get in trouble for not having my math homework. Amanda ignored me.

But at lunch, she and her friends giggled in my direction and headed straight for the cafeteria. That put a funny feeling in my stomach. I walked toward my locker.

On the floor in front of our locker was a big mess. My peanut butter and jelly sandwich was there, smeared across the ground in streaks of purple and brown. And on top of the gooey heap was one of my extra gym sneakers. A piece of paper stuck out of the sneaker, the words visible from several feet away: SCAB SANDWICH.

For a minute, I couldn't think about anything but the hand-clapping song: *So she made me a scab sandwich . . . mustard on top . . . eagle eyeballs . . . and camel snot . . .*

Then I heard people around me start to laugh. My red face gave away that the sandwich was mine.

"Elise? Elise?"

Caroline.

"I—I need to clean my sneaker," I stammered. I reached down and freed it from the sticky sandwich. I flipped it over to see all the grooves filled with goop. I crumpled the note.

In the bathroom, I wet a paper towel and carefully wiped out the rubber ridges of my sneaker.

Caroline came into the bathroom and washed peanut butter off her hands. She must have cleaned up the sandwich. That made me want to cry or hug her, but I concentrated on not being upset. I couldn't open my mouth, because the lump in my throat was growing bigger and bigger and carrying me dangerously closer to crying.

"Has . . . anything like this . . . happened before?" Caroline asked.

I still couldn't speak, but I nodded. She looked confused as she thought about my answer.

I left the bathroom ahead of her and went to the school-lunch line. I handed over a five-dollar bill and got a tray of soggy veggies, a small pizza with more dry sauce than cheese, and a chocolate pudding cup. I brought the tray to the table where Franklin was sitting.

"Elise!" he said. "You're late. Why do you have school lunch?"

I still couldn't talk. I tore off a bit of pizza and put it into my mouth, chewing carefully.

"What happened?" Franklin asked.

I didn't answer. I watched Caroline walk into the cafeteria, head over to the table with Amanda and her friends, and sit down.

I Wonder Whether Grown-Ups Understand at All

When I got home, Ava was the only person I wanted to be with. She was the perfect size for holding. She couldn't ask me what was wrong or whether school had been good. She didn't react to the fact that I was crying as I held her against me. Babies cry all the time. Crying must not seem like a big deal to them. And she couldn't offer advice, so I wouldn't have to explain why the advice wouldn't work. Or admit that it was good advice and find the courage to go through with it. She just let me feel sad until I was done crying.

Annie came into the room.

"Elise?" she asked. "Um, Cricket, honey?"

I didn't answer. She left and came back with Uncle Hugh. Annie gently lifted Ava from me. The baby made a noise, but Annie shushed her and pressed a pacifier past her lips.

"What's wrong?" Uncle Hugh smoothed the loose hair off my forehead.

I started crying again. Uncle Hugh held me, just like I had been holding Ava.

• • •

"Every day for three months someone at school has tried to ruin your lunch?"

We were all at the dinner table, with Ava asleep in her carrier seat on the floor. Bow-tie mac-and-cheese, pork chops, peas, applesauce. But no one had touched the food.

"Yep."

"Why didn't you tell us?" Aunt Bessie said.

I shrugged.

"Where does this happen?" Uncle Hugh asked. "In the cafeteria?"

"In our locker."

"Why don't you just not leave your lunch there? Or get a hard plastic lunch box?"

"Well, one, there's just as much chance of it getting squished if I carry it around or keep it in my backpack all day.

"Two, I have a right to be able to keep things safely in my locker.

"Three, because I don't want to have a baby lunch box.

"And four, if someone really wants to wreck your food, they can just open the lunch box."

"That's true." Uncle Hugh got a cold cream soda and handed it to me. "You do have a right to use your own locker. You know what to do when someone isn't treating you well at school, right?"

Punch? Kick? Bite?

"Tell a grown-up," I answered.

Aunt Bessie nodded. "You can always tell a grown-up."

"You *can't*," I said. "Then you get in more trouble with the other kids. It isn't cool."

"There are more important things," Uncle Hugh said. "Like being able to eat your lunch. Like feeling safe and comfortable at school every day."

How do you explain to your uncle that being cool and feeling safe and comfortable at school were really the same thing?

"Besides, I told a teacher a couple times, and she didn't really care."

"Well, why didn't you tell *us*?"

"I didn't want to talk about Amanda at home. I try not to *think* about Amanda at home."

"I just don't understand why you didn't tell us," Uncle Hugh said.

I didn't say anything. Why would I be expected to talk about something that made me look like such a loser? Why would I want to bring that feeling home?

"Please eat some dinner." Aunt Bessie picked up her fork. "You haven't had enough to eat today. You might feel better."

I cut off a tiny bite of pork chop, moved the meat to my mouth, and chewed it.

The phone rang and Annie answered.

"Hang on a minute, okay?" She covered the mouthpiece. "Elise, honey, it's Caroline. Do you want to talk to her?"

I shook my head. Why did Caroline help me and then go sit with Amanda? How could she be friends with both of us?

Annie spoke into the phone again. "Elise is at dinner right now. She'll see you at school tomorrow, okay? . . . Goodbye."

"If you're not taking phone calls," Aunt Bessie said, "are you taking mail?"

"I never get mail."

"You did today." She went to the mail pile, fished out an envelope, and set it in front of me. There was no return name or address, and mine were taped on in newspaper-cutout letters. The postmark said California.

"Who would send me mail? I don't even know anyone in California."

I slid my fingers under the paper to tear open the flap. No note. I tipped the envelope. A metallic *clunk* sounded as a key hit the table.

We all stared at it.

Aunt Bessie picked up her fork. "Eat everything on your plate, and then try out the key, if you want. Don't forget your homework. Tomorrow will be easier if you get it done."

I nodded and managed to eat my dinner.

The room behind the door matched the one about me and Dad. There was a book on the floor with a note on top and photos on the wall—of a growing boy, and then of a man— Uncle Hugh.

The note said, UNDERSTAND THOSE YOU LOVE. I picked up the book.

I took the book to Mom's comfy chair and curled up.

Uncle Hugh had been twelve years older than Dad. That's a lot older. The first pages of the book were Dad's earliest memories of Uncle Hugh. Uncle Hugh took good care of his brothers, but in a way that was sort of silly and fun. Like the time Dad learned to swim because Uncle Hugh just threw him in the lake. Dad floundered until Hugh went in to get him. After that, Dad wasn't afraid of the water anymore, because he had been underneath and nothing bad had happened. When Uncle Hugh found that Dad had been downstairs in the middle of the night on Christmas Eve and unwrapped all the presents, he stayed up for hours rewrapping everything. And when Uncle Hugh took both of his brothers camping, Dad got so afraid that there might be bears that Uncle Hugh let him cuddle up in his own sleeping bag with him for the night.

The entries started to be more about Hugh on his own.

Uncle Hugh had grown up with a boy named Joshua who was his best friend. They were in a band together in high school, and were going to enlist in the army together, but then Uncle Hugh decided to go to college instead. Joshua enlisted and ended up being killed. A little piece of Hugh was missing after that.

When Uncle Hugh first lived alone, he got a dog and named her Sadie. Sadie went just about everywhere with him. She eventually got old and sick with tumors and Uncle Hugh had to put her to sleep.

I couldn't read any more about Uncle Hugh then. He was such a nice guy, he shouldn't have had so many sad things happen. And here he was stuck with mopey old me, the girl nobody liked and who couldn't do anything right.

I remembered what Aunt Bessie'd said about home-work. If I did at least some of it, maybe tomorrow would be better. And while I worked I could just think about the assignments.

Uncle Hugh found me sitting on the porch after I said I was leaving for school in the morning. He sat down next to me. "What are you up to, Cricket?"

"Nothing."

"Why aren't you on your way to the bus?"

I picked at the frayed end of my shoelace, where the plastic had cracked off. "I'm not ready yet."

Uncle Hugh swatted my hand away from the shoelace and retied my sneaker for me like I was a little girl. "There. Ready now?"

I shook my head.

Uncle Hugh released my sneaker. "I know it's hard to go to school when kids aren't being nice to you. I do know."

"It isn't just that," I admitted.

"Oh? What else?"

"It's not like anyone ever asked you if you wanted this. Me, I mean."

"How do you know no one asked us?"

Aunt Bessie stepped out onto the porch and handed me a brown paper bag. "You forgot this." She had taken extra care in packing my lunch nicely. She had even taken a pink marker and written, *Have a happy lunch, sweet,* enclosed in a heart, with a smiley face, to boot.

"Thanks, Aunt Bessie."

Uncle Hugh helped me get up.

"Remember that telling a grown-up at school could help you," he said. "That's the best option. We know you'll do the right thing."

I put on a defiant face as I approached the locker. It was my locker. I had a right to use it.

"Cute," Amanda declared when she saw my lovey lunch from Aunt Bessie. "Why don't you put your lunch up top today?"

Had a teacher spotted what had happened in the hallway yesterday? Had Caroline talked to her? Maybe that was why she went to sit with her.

"Okay," I said, willing to see if today would be different.

Amanda smiled at me as I opened my backpack and took out my math book.

"Let me put that away for you," she said. She took the heavy book from me, and set it on the top shelf. Then she slid it all the way back, catching my lunch and mashing it against the wall. She shut the locker door. "Have a good day, Scabular." She walked away.

The time had come to take action.

We Are All in Deep Dog Poo

There are several ways to retaliate when someone squashes your lunch every day.

You can steal her lunch; fill your own lunch bag with something vile, so that when she squashes it, her stuff gets ruined; or fill her lunch bag with shaving cream.

We settled on option three.

"I don't know where we'd hide a stolen lunch. And putting something gross in your own lunch bag and letting her smash it could ruin your books," Franklin reasoned.

Eventually we had the plan all figured out.

We would go to our lockers like any other day.

Then I'd be in class with Amanda all morning. I wouldn't even be able to go to the bathroom (Amanda needed to have me in her sight at all times, to keep her from suspecting us).

Franklin would sneak out during second period, when he *didn't* have class with Amanda, make sure no one was in the hallway, and take care of everything.

And Amanda would finally know what it was like to have a ruined lunch.

Aunt Bessie came into my room at bedtime. I had my knees up in front of me with my math book on them, trying to quickly finish up the problems.

"You and Franklin sure had your heads together up in that library. Working on homework?"

"Yeah," I lied.

"How did it go with your lunch today?"

"Fine."

"So you were able to enjoy your lunch? It didn't get wrecked?"

"No, it did."

Aunt Bessie sat down. "So then why is that fine? It doesn't sound fine. Did you tell a teacher?"

"I already told you teachers don't care." I finished the last problem and shut the book. Aunt Bessie took it from me and started stroking my hair.

"Telling a teacher again won't be so bad," she said. "It will make things better. You'll see. Tomorrow things will be better. There's my girl."

I let her talk and talk but didn't listen.

Our plan was not on Uncle Hugh and Aunt Bessie's List of Helpful Suggestions.

Luckily, they wouldn't find out about it.

Franklin brought the shaving cream. His mother's. It was pink and smelled like berries.

"Why didn't you bring your dad's?"

"Dad would notice it was gone. He has just one can he uses every day, but Mom has twenty-seven bottles of stuff in the bathroom. Well, now twenty-six."

"What if something goes wrong?" I asked.

"Nothing will go wrong," Franklin promised. "And if the authorities interrogate you, just say, 'Why would I vandalize something in my own locker?'"

"I'm going to be interrogated?"

Franklin shrugged. "Maybe. You'll probably be suspect number one. But you'll have been with Amanda all morning. And they've got no reason to suspect me. We should both be safe."

The first-period bell rang, so I ran to my locker and dropped off my lunch (which was squished a few seconds later) and half my books and then headed to class with Amanda a few feet behind me.

"Are you okay?" Caroline asked when I sat down. "You look all red."

I ignored her, like I had all day yesterday.

We listened to Mrs. Wakefield explain our new unit on symbolism. Then she passed out poems for us to read aloud. Language arts finally ended and we split up for math, science, or social studies and headed out into the hall. Franklin gave me a small salute when no one was looking.

After fourth period we headed to our lockers on the way to the cafeteria. I was a little shaky as I fished my squashed lunch out from the bottom of the locker. Amanda daintily reached up to get hers from the top shelf. I looked up just enough to see that the bag was a bit puffier than usual.

"Why are you *always* in the way?" she barked. "Get *up*."

While I got up, I slammed our locker door—before her lunch had entirely cleared the metal frame.

Plpphpht!

The bag exploded. Amanda and I both got *covered* in pink, fragrant shaving cream. The other kids cleared a circle around us and began to clap.

Amanda shrieked as she wiped shaving cream from her eyes. "I'll kill you!" She threw herself at me.

"What did *I* do?" I hadn't planned on a shaving-cream explosion. I shoved her to keep her off me, but she grabbed me by the shoulders. Soon we were both spinning around, sliding in the shaving cream and yelling at each other.

And that was how I landed in the principal's office.

When you're sitting in the principal's office awaiting your fate, time seems to pass incredibly slowly. I could hear every click of the clock over the desk. The smell of fake berries on my sweatshirt was almost unbearable.

Ms. Hadley walked in and sat down behind her desk. She contemplated both of us. Finally, she said, "Amanda, why don't you tell me what happened?"

"I went to take out my lunch and Elise tried to shut my hand in the locker. She got my lunch instead and shaving cream went everywhere."

"Why was there shaving cream in your lunch?"

"I don't know."

"Why do you *think* there was shaving cream in your lunch?"

"Elise put it there."

Ms. Hadley didn't react to that hypothesis, but she put up a hand to keep me from speaking.

"So then you verbally threatened and attacked her?"

Amanda couldn't come up with anything to say.

Ms. Hadley said, "Elise, why don't you tell me what happened?"

"Amanda said I was in the way, so I tried to get up and shut our locker. I didn't know her lunch was there."

"Did you know there was shaving cream in it?"

"No."

I felt my fingers start to tremble against the legs of my jeans. *Be cool, be cool,* I willed them. *Be still.*

"We'll talk about the shaving cream in a minute," Ms. Hadley said. "My first concern is the physical fighting. You were seen fighting, both of you. Is that true?"

I looked at my lap and mumbled, "Yes." I was surprised to hear an echo from the chair next to me.

"Did you know that fighting is grounds for suspension?"

We shook our heads.

"As is verbally threatening another student, Amanda." Ms. Hadley paused. "I don't think I am going to suspend either of you, though. Neither of you is injured and neither of you has engaged in physical fighting before."

Before relief had time to reach all the way to my trembling fingertips, Ms. Hadley added, "However . . .

"I am very curious as to where the shaving cream came from. It seems to me that shaving cream in a lunch is a prank, which is something premeditated with the intent to humiliate another student. That seems a more severe offense than loss of temper, and I won't tolerate it. Amanda, tell me again how you believe shaving cream got in your lunch."

"Elise put it there."

"Why do you suspect Elise?"

"My lunch was in our locker."

Crap.

"Elise, how do you think the shaving cream got there?"

Be cool. "I don't know."

Ms. Hadley was silent for a minute. Then she said, "I take things like this very seriously. You really don't know how shaving cream got in Amanda's lunch?"

"I don't. I was in class all morning. Ask my teachers."

"Are you two the only students who know the combination to your locker?"

About a thousand thoughts whirred rapidly through my head.

Tell her how horrible Amanda's been all year. Tell her about the prank she played on you just a couple days ago.

Grown-ups don't care. She'll just give you a list of grown-up solutions again.

Amanda would be even worse *from now on if I did that right in front of her.*

There's a way out.

But it's against every kid rule.

"Elise." Ms. Hadley halted all the whirring. "You are facing suspension."

I couldn't do it. I couldn't rat out Franklin. But I looked at Amanda, whose face had twisted into an evil smirk.

"There *is* someone else who knows the combination," Amanda said. "Elise's *boyfriend*. He gets her work if she's out sick."

"He's not my boyfriend," I mumbled, staring down at my jeans. My heart thundered in panic. What had Franklin planned to do with the empty shaving-cream can? Was it in his backpack? His locker? A trash bin in a classroom? Franklin was thorough, right? He took care of details like that?

"Who is this friend?" Ms. Hadley asked.

"Franklin White." Amanda was very excited. She knew that this would be the best way to get me back.

Ms. Hadley paged someone to go get Franklin out of class.

When Franklin arrived, he seemed to have trembly fingers, too.

"Do you know why I have called you in here?"

"No." Franklin sat down.

"Do you know why Elise is here?"

"No."

"There was an incident involving Elise, Amanda, and a great deal of shaving cream. Were you aware of that?"

"No." I think he made a tiny mistake here. A friend who didn't know that I was involved in an incident with Amanda and shaving cream would have acted more surprised and concerned.

"It seems that there are only two people who could have

played a prank on Amanda like the one that was performed today, and both of those people are sitting in front of me. If it's true, Franklin, that you had nothing to do with it, the blame shall fall solely on Elise. Would that be fair? We are talking about suspension."

"I confess!" Franklin wailed dramatically. "I confess!" He threw his arms up and then slumped in his chair.

"You did it?"

"Yes. I filled Amanda's lunch with shaving cream as an act of retaliation for the cruelty she has shown my friend Elise from the very first day of school."

"I see," Ms. Hadley said. "No such cruelty has been brought to my attention before. While normally I would suggest that students work out their differences, I feel in this case that I will reassign your locker, Elise, to prevent another scene like today's." She wrote something on a slip of paper and handed it to me. "Bring that to the secretaries and they will reassign you."

"Now, as for the matter of this prank," she continued. "Franklin, did you act alone, or did you and Elise act together?"

"I . . . I acted alone," Franklin said.

"Elise?"

This was the part when I was supposed to jump in and help Franklin, the friend who had tried to help me. This was the part when I would share the blame.

I tried not to look at Amanda.

How bad would things get if I said I was behind it? Even if I didn't admit to it, Amanda would still assume I'd done it anyway, right? We wouldn't be sharing a locker anymore, but she could still do awful things.

What about everyone else, though? Would things go better with them if I didn't have Franklin to make me look so silly? Hadn't all the trouble started because people thought we were both little kids, Elise and Franklin, a pair, together all the time, exactly alike? I thought about the playing pretend and my injuries and the Star Wars toys all over the hallway. I could show now that I wasn't so tied to him, that I wasn't just a baby like him.

I looked at Franklin, who would never let me down, and I suddenly felt so angry at him. He trusted me completely, and that hurt. I didn't deserve that kind of trust.

My mouth stayed shut.

"Elise didn't have anything to do with it?" Ms. Hadley turned to Franklin.

"No," Franklin said. "I acted entirely alone."

"Elise? Did you help?"

I said, "No."

And Franklin got suspended by himself.

I Am Garbage

I curled up in my bed as soon as I got home.

Aunt Bessie found me there a little while later. "Are you okay?"

I didn't answer.

She tried again. "Lise?"

She gave me another minute, then she said, "School called. Are you in your bed because you got in a fight? Are you hurt?"

"I am garbage."

"You aren't garbage."

"I *am*. Garbage."

I was garbage for knowing Franklin wouldn't turn me in and saying nothing. For wanting so much to please Uncle Hugh and Aunt Bessie but not taking their advice.

"Why didn't you talk to a grown-up before fighting?" Aunt Bessie asked. It sounded like she was asking herself, not me.

"When we tried to tell Ms. Hadley what Amanda had been doing, she didn't really care."

"Did you tell her before you were in the fight, or after?"

I didn't answer.

"They made me move lockers."

I'd loaded up all my books and gym stuff and carried them to my new locker, in a tucked-away corner beyond the eighth graders whose last names start with Z. A girl with a side pony and a tutu-material black skirt gave me a funny look as I fit the lock on the door and practiced the new combination.

"How do you feel about that?" Aunt Bessie asked.

"Kind of . . . lonely," I said. "But nobody will smash my lunch."

"That's a good thing, right?" she asked.

"Amanda was being mean to me. *She* should have been moved."

"Everything changes when you physically fight back," Aunt Bessie pointed out. "Then you're equally at fault."

I sighed and slumped my face back against my pillow. Aunt Bessie squeezed her hands together.

"I didn't realize how bad things were."

I wanted to tell her that that wasn't her fault, it was mine. But again, I kept my mouth shut.

Later, Uncle Hugh came by.

"Cricket?"

"What?"

"What are you doing?"

"Staring at the wall."

"Good," he said. "I don't feel bad interrupting that. Sit

up." Uncle Hugh set a steaming plate on my desk. "Baked ziti tonight." He paused. "Franklin's mother called. She says he's upset and won't talk about it. She doesn't think it's just the suspension, because Franklin said he did the wrong thing and the punishment is fair. So . . ."

"It's me," I admitted. "I've upset everyone. Even Aunt Bessie."

"It's pretty hard to do that."

"Are you upset?" I asked.

"I'm not pleased," he said. "Why don't you give Franklin a call?"

I shook my head. I'd made a decision. I knew I'd lost him. That had been the idea.

I just hadn't realized how awful it would feel. I thought I would feel free. Maybe that would come later.

"You should finish reading this." Uncle Hugh held out the book from the barn, the one all about him.

"Did you read it?" I asked, surprised.

"I did. You should, too."

I opened to where I had left off, and read several little stories about how Hugh had been part of my life before Dad died. About how he took me on a trip to the zoo in the rain. About how he let me stand on a table to build a block tower seven feet high. About how he and Bessie came to live in our house to help out when Dad started going to the hospital.

And then,

. . . when Hugh met Bessie, things were just perfect. They got married within two years of meeting each other and talked about the family they would have, but a few years passed and it turned out that Bessie couldn't have children.

I thought a long time about who I should appoint as your guardian. I knew that if I left you with my brother Beau and his family, you'd grow up with brothers like I did, and your mother and I had always meant for you to have siblings. But my heart was telling me that you belonged with Hugh and Bessie. They always should have been parents, and, in some light, because Life seems to have a mind of its own, maybe you were destined to be their chance to have a family.

I found Aunt Bessie in the living room.

Aunt Bessie never really sits around. She always seems so busy.

"What are you doing?" I asked.

"Just reading before I clean up from dinner. The dishes are soaking."

"I'll help."

"Okay." She put her tired red leather bookmark in place and closed the book.

"Or . . . I could do all the dishes."

I walked over to her, climbed into her lap. I'm much too

big for that; hadn't done it in years and years, couldn't even remember doing it, really. But I sat sideways with my legs on the couch. I put my arms around her neck and rested my head on her shoulder.

She slipped her arms around me and held on.

"I'm really sorry," I said.

"I know."

"You're a good mom."

Aunt Bessie nodded, gave me a kiss on the cheek, and held me, just a little tighter than before.

No More Franklin

They made me go to school the next morning, even though I said I'd rather stay home. *Especially* because I said I'd rather stay home, because I said I wanted to pretend I was suspended, too.

It was torture.

Franklin wasn't on the school bus, just like I knew he wouldn't be. Were his parents mad at him for getting suspended?

Franklin probably hated me.

A big, empty table waited for me at lunch.

I watched the kids coming into the cafeteria. Soon Caroline arrived, heading in Amanda's direction. But then she passed table after table until she ended up at mine.

"Can I sit with you?"

"No. I'm pretty sure in a minute or two this table will be full."

"I've been trying to talk to you for days."

I ignored her and went back to my sandwich. Chew, chew. Chew, chew.

"Look, you're not the only person who's just ditched your oldest friend. I want to talk to you!" Caroline looked mad. That was new. Well, I was super-mad myself.

But it didn't look like she was going anywhere. And what did she mean, ditched her oldest friend? I sighed. "It's a free country."

Caroline sat across from me and took out her turkey and cheese, her container of peaches, her Snapple.

"Why aren't you sitting with them?"

"I've been trying to tell you. After the other day, what Amanda did to you, we had a big fight."

Chew, chew. Chew, chew.

"I thought I could be friends with everyone I wanted to, that I could go between as long as I didn't get in anyone's way. But Amanda . . . Anyway, I told her I wasn't going to hang out with her anymore."

"So you gave up a lousy friend. Big deal."

"It is! We've been friends forever. And it also means I lose Kate and Lindsay, and Brennan and his friends, because Amanda's always with them. It's a lot."

Maybe that was a big deal. Maybe it was a big deal to decide to walk away from your friends, whatever the reason.

"So anyway, I wanted to say that I'm sorry. I didn't know that Amanda was being so mean to you. I thought it was just some name-calling. I didn't know it was every day, and I didn't know about your lunch. And then it took a while for it to sink in, what was really going on. I couldn't believe it, how much she'd changed. I didn't want to."

I was listening to her now, but something still seemed

167

wrong. "So you think you can say all that and we'll be friends, just like that?"

"Hey. You don't have the best track record, either. Look at Franklin."

My ears felt very hot.

"But, whatever. You've always been nice to me. Even if you're grumpy today." Caroline decided to eat her sandwich then, as if she'd finally been invited to lunch. "I think you guys will work it out, though."

"No," I said. "It didn't make sense anymore, being friends."

"Make sense to who?"

I thought of the raw feeling I'd had in my stomach since I'd left Ms. Hadley's office. I wondered if Franklin had one, too. If he did, his was probably worse. Did he feel all ripped up? Squished really small? Smashed with the heel of a shoe, like a bug?

What had really gone wrong with me and Franklin? And when? Why had being his friend gone from feeling just fine to feeling bad? And if it had felt bad to be his friend, why did it feel worse not to be?

Caroline and I ate in silence. All that time she'd sat with Amanda when Amanda was being mean to me, and now she was willing to sit with me after I'd been horrible to Franklin. Maybe that didn't make her awful. Maybe she stuck with people, gave them chances. Maybe that was what friends did. Franklin had given me a lot of chances.

"What about the shaving cream in Amanda's lunch? Doesn't that bother you?"

Caroline shrugged. "It's not like you started it. She had it coming. Did Franklin really do that all by himself?"

Well, Franklin really *had* taken care of everything, but . . . "He did it for me."

"Why can't you be friends anymore? Are you sure?"

I didn't feel sure about anything.

"Are you worried?" I asked.

"About . . . ?"

"What Amanda will do to you."

"Oh no."

"No?"

Caroline shook her head. Then she tapped it.

"I've got six years of secrets up here. I don't think she'll be trying anything on me."

Aunt Bessie picked me up after detention. Amanda and I had earned ourselves a week's worth. Uncle Hugh was waiting on the porch when I got home.

"How'd it go?" he asked, patting the blue-painted boards next to him for me to sit down.

I dropped my backpack and sat. "I had to scrape the gum off the bottom of desks with Amanda. For an hour."

"Did you talk? Work things out?"

"No. She tried to leave gum wads where I could step in them."

"Things will get better," Uncle Hugh said. "*You* will make them better."

"I can't make anything better."

"On the contrary," said Uncle Hugh. "You're the only one who can. Start by calling Franklin."

"Are you going to make me do that?" I asked.

"I'm not going to make you do anything. What kind of apology is 'My uncle said I had to call you'? Anything you do should come from you."

Franklin was at school the next day. I left a seat open next to me on the bus, but he didn't sit there. He passed my table at lunch, too. Those were the hardest tests yet. But I didn't call after him. I didn't try to explain. The next couple days after that went pretty much the same way.

After my last detention I walked to Leonard's. In front of the hardware store was a familiar car. Mrs. White's.

I thought about running away, but I was already too close. She spotted me when she climbed out of the car.

"Elise!"

"Uh, hi, Mrs. White. What are you doing here?"

"I had to find a parking space. Franklin's at the orthodontist"—she gestured to the dentist's office next door—"getting fitted for braces. He has to have two teeth pulled. But you probably know all about that already."

Actually, I didn't know anything about Franklin getting braces.

I thought about the first time Franklin lost a tooth, in kindergarten. I wiggled it out for him. He cried when he saw all the blood, so I reminded him that it was good to lose a tooth. You got a treat at home under your pillow.

Would Mrs. White give him a treat for having them yanked out at age eleven?

She was standing next to me now.

"So, Elise . . . What exactly happened between you and Franklin?"

"Nothing."

"Really? Nothing?"

"I have to go inside."

I turned, but Mrs. White started up again. "I know he acts like a tough guy, but he's really hurting."

In what universe would Franklin be called a "tough guy"? Well, he hadn't been acting upset at school. Maybe that was what she meant. What about at home? Maybe he still wasn't talking about it there, either.

"Why don't you come over for dinner?" she offered. "We can all sit down together and talk things out."

"I can't." Would Franklin really be eating dinner with bloody gauze in his mouth? Would he feel like talking? And what would dinner be? Plain boiled veggies over steamed rice?

"Maybe another night, then? Tomorrow?"

"I said I can't."

I knew she wanted to help, but it made me angry. This was what was wrong to begin with. Franklin was a baby. She treated him like a baby. Let him take care of his own problems.

• • •

I meant to do my homework. I really did. But I went to my bedroom and lay down with my head on the pillow. I reached my hands underneath it to scrunch it properly, and felt something small and metal.

No way.

I closed my hand around the key and headed out to the barn.

Only three doors left.

The one the key fit opened to a tiny room. The walls were covered with photographs. The name of each place was written on the matting around each picture. Geneva, Switzerland, and Beijing, China, and Johannesburg, South Africa, and about a hundred other places. One frame didn't have a picture in it, but words: *When I grew up, I was going to be an explorer.*

My dad hadn't been an explorer, though. He'd worked in a bank.

The room was different from Mom's and Uncle Hugh's not just because of the pictures. Their rooms were about what someone else thought was a good idea to know about them, but Dad's room was what he wanted me to know about himself.

This time, the note said, TREASURE YOUR LIFE.

The part of Dad who had been a little boy had left a train set in the middle of the floor. The part who had been a teenager had left three shelves of trophies, certificates, and ribbons—sports awards, science fair medals. The college student left a bookshelf of notebooks and papers.

There was a small journal explaining about him being sick. I had only heard that it was a kind of cancer that had spread even though they were trying to fight it. He got it about a year after my mom died. When he had started acting tired and sick, everyone had just assumed it was grief. But it wasn't. It was a relief to know that Dad had died from something that didn't have to do with me; it wasn't my fault. It had nothing to do with being sad about Mom.

There were a few scrapbooks. I really liked the one full of pictures of Dad, Uncle Hugh, and Uncle Beau as kids. They were doing happy things: playing at a lake, playing in the snow, fishing, riding bicycles. . . . Sometimes there was a fourth boy in the pictures. I'd have to ask Uncle Hugh who that was.

Another book had wedding photos. Mom's bridesmaids had been in blue—a younger Aunt Bessie was one—and Uncle Hugh and Uncle Beau were Dad's groomsmen. The best man looked familiar.

I took the two scrapbooks to Uncle Hugh in his workshop.

"Yeah, that's Leonard," he confirmed.

"So are all these . . . ?" I flipped through the pictures with the fourth boy.

"All Leonard. Aw, look at him little. Look at all of us. Where'd you get this?"

"Upstairs. The next room's about Dad."

"The next room? How'd you get into it?"

"A key showed up."

"Jiminy, Cricket."

"Jiminy, Uncle."

He was studying the pictures, so I let him hold on to the books and went back upstairs.

The next book I found was all about Dad and Leonard. The two of them had had such a good time. It made me miss Franklin. And it made me miss Dad a little.

Which gave me an idea.

"Hey, Leonard," I said, surprising him where he was stamping prices on boxes of nails.

"Hey there, Cricket. Alone again?"

"Yeah." I followed him back to the storage room. "I'm here to call in my birthday present: one day-trip to a place of my choice."

"Where do you want to go?"

"The old lake."

"You do? When we could go see a 3-D movie and eat a big bucket of popcorn and wear funny glasses?"

"Yep."

"When we could drive into the city to go to the aquarium and watch the sharks get fed?"

"Yep."

"When we could wait until spring and go to the amusement park and eat too much cotton candy and ride on the roller coaster and listen to me complain about how my body's too old for those things?"

"Yep."

"You know we'll do all of those things anyway."

"Yep."

"When do you want to do this?"

"Next week? We have days off for Thanksgiving. You usually spend time with us then anyway."

"We'll see. I'd need time to get ready for a trip like this."

"It's not far, right?"

"Not distance-far," said Leonard. "Another kind of far."

Thanksgiving with Leonard

Uncle Hugh knocked on my door.

"Are you sick? It's noon." He came over, gently tugged on my ponytail, and put his hand on my forehead.

"No fever," he announced. "You sure you feel okay?"

"I feel blaaaahhh."

"I didn't know twelve-year-olds could feel blah on Thanksgiving."

"Twelve-year-olds feel whatever they want, whenever they want."

Uncle Hugh laughed. "Sit up."

I sat up.

"You have pillow creases all over your face." Uncle Hugh smoothed away the hair that had fallen out of my ponytail. "Tell me why you've spent this wonderful day with your face in a pillow."

"I'm tired," I said, "and so happy not to be at school."

Thanksgiving made me want Christmas to come soon, but I wondered if it would feel lonely this year, without Franklin. Who would make his hot cocoa? *No milk*, he always reminds me. *I know!* I always say. And what about candy canes? There aren't good ones at his house. His mom's had the same candy canes on their Christmas tree for ten years. Nobody's allowed to eat them; they're for "decoration."

"Get up," Uncle Hugh said. "Get dressed. Beau, Sally, and your cousins will be here soon and Aunt Bessie needs your help in the kitchen. She wants to make an apple pie while the turkey thaws."

"Okay. But I'm not getting dressed up."

"Okay. Make sure your sneaks are sloppily tied and your socks don't match, and for heaven's sakes, don't comb your hair."

"Deal."

I'd never made an apple pie before. It took way longer than applesauce. We peeled the apples, cut the apples, sugared the apples—then there was the crust, which was a whole other story. Aunt Bessie let me take some of the leftover dough to decorate the top of the pie; I made leaves and apples with cookie-cutters.

Annie mixed the stuffing for the turkey. Ava was in her high chair, in a happy, gurgly mood. After I finished the pie, I took charge of entertaining Ava. I put a metal mixing bowl on my head, tapped it with a wooden spoon, and made a funny face to go along with each tap. She let out bursts of laughing squeals.

"Hey, Cricket."

I turned around. "Hi, Leonard."

"Ready to go?" he asked.

"Right now?"

"Yes, right now."

"Aunt Bessie asked me to help her. . . ."

"You helped," she said. "We knew he was coming. That's part of why we needed to get you dressed."

They're all so sneaky.

The drive to the old lake took an hour. I'd expected a sandy beach, but after parking we had a bit of a hike. The path was covered with brown, crunchy leaves, and the only way you could really see it was because the trees were a little farther apart. But Leonard knew the way.

"There she is," Leonard said finally. "We'd walk up here, sit on these rocks, and just talk."

"Okay." We sat, but didn't start talking. I looked out at the smooth water, dark and far away.

We must have been thinking about the same person.

Would the water freeze soon? Did Dad and Leonard go ice-skating here in the winter? Maybe they swam there in the summer, or looked for frogs like me and Franklin liked to do.

I sighed. "It must be lonely, when your best friend is gone forever."

"It can be," Leonard said.

"Were you guys friends till the end?"

"Till the end."

"So you were friends for years and years?"

"Our whole lives. Or, maybe it makes more sense to say, for your dad's whole life."

"Did you fight, ever?"

"Sure."

I was quiet. Leonard said, "Think Franklin'll be coming by the store with you soon?"

"No," I said, in a tiny voice.

Leonard took a turn being quiet. Then he said, "A good friend is one of the hardest things to keep in this life. Don't forget that sometimes you have to work at it."

But I *had* forgotten, before I'd even learned.

"I don't feel different," I said finally. "I thought I would feel different. You said you always felt different after you went to the lake. I thought it would help, to do something that worked for Dad."

"Just going to the old lake doesn't fix anything, you know. It's how you change at the lake. You go away, think about things, and you come back a little bit different. Only you can change what you are."

That sounded like things Uncle Hugh had been saying and Dad had written.

I let Leonard's last sentence repeat in my head. I let it whir and whirl. I let the wind swirl it around and around me and then carry it away. It carried it out across the smooth water of the lake, making ripples that were not smooth, but became smoothed out again.

"Do you like what I am?"

"What?"

"Do you like what I am?"

"I always love our Cricket, whatever she is." He paused. "The better question is, do *you* like what you are?"

I waited, then said, "I don't."

"I want to hear the whole thing, from the beginning, up to how we got here right now. Start talking, Cricket."

Something to Believe In

On Sunday morning, I found another key.

This one was on my dresser next to some clean socks Aunt Bessie had dropped off. Was it from her? I doubted it, for some reason. It could have been there for days.

After this one there would be just one more key. And maybe then I would learn who the mysterious key-giver was. Who would send a key from California? The person who left all the rest of the keys had to be someone who could get in the house—or somebody already in it. Unless the keys were coming from Somewhere Else . . . through a time warp or by angel messenger or . . .

I pushed those thoughts out of my mind to deal with later and headed outside.

This room looked like the library, except smaller, without the desk.

Why would Dad give me *another* room full of books? But the room had books from floor to ceiling anyway, with the exception of a mirror sitting on one of the shelves. I scanned some of the titles. *Taoism. Native American Myths. The Historical Jesus.* Nothing interesting. I pulled one off the shelf. It looked like hard reading.

The message on the floor said, BELIEVE.

The books were all things to believe in.

The mirror was kind of a weird addition. I stared at my reflection.

And suddenly, that made sense, too.

I was also supposed to believe in *myself*.

At lunch, Franklin walked by our table, looking for a place to sit. Caroline waved at him. He waved back but kept going.

Caroline turned to me. "What are you working on?" She looked at the loose-leaf paper and mechanical pencil I was hiding under the table.

"The poetry assignment," I said. Our usual paragraph assignment had turned into poems for the rest of the unit. "I'm really sick of writing poems. I just don't get what they should be about."

"What have your other ones been about?" Caroline asked.

"Dumb things. Springtime. Winter."

"Do you really care about winter?"

I shook my head.

Caroline looked over a few tables, where Franklin was eating a sandwich (probably bologna with yellow mustard) and talking with Diana, who was in an orange sweatshirt with a black cat on it, looking like Halloween.

Then Caroline started reading, letting me do my home-work. I liked having her just sit next to me while the thoughts whirred in my head.

I decided to finish my homework at home and started to eat. My peanut butter sandwich that was not flattened or smooshed or crushed or hurt in any way. It still stuck to the roof of my mouth and in my throat just as much.

I looked around for Amanda. She was several tables away, laughing with Kate and Lindsay and a couple boys.

"What's Amanda's deal, anyway?" I asked.

"I don't know," Caroline said. "She wasn't always like this."

"I saw her with her brother once. He and his friends weren't that nice to her."

"No, they aren't."

"But just because someone is mean to her doesn't give her the right to be mean to other people."

Then a funny feeling squirmed inside me. *Like I was to Franklin?*

The truth was, it wasn't just the not-fessing-up in the principal's office that was wrong between me and Franklin. I hadn't been nice to him all year. I called him names. I didn't like to do things with him the way I had before because I was worried about what other people would think. He embar-rassed me, even though I should have been happy to have such a good friend. I really hadn't been a good friend to him for a long, long time.

• • •

I took a deep breath and dialed.

Mrs. White answered. "Hello?"

"Hi. Is Franklin there?"

"Oh, hi, Elise. Let me go see if I can find him."

I waited. She would know exactly where he was; she meant "Let me see if he wants to talk to you."

"I'm sorry," she said. "He's doing homework right now and doesn't want to be interrupted. Maybe try him tomorrow?"

"Uh, okay, thanks," I managed to say. "Bye."

"Oh, and Elise?"

"Yeah?"

"Thank you for calling."

I hung up.

A Lifetime Supply of Questions

When Mrs. Wakefield said it was time to have someone share her poem, I expected her to call on Caroline. She called on her almost every week.

"Elise, come up and share with us."

I was so surprised I stayed in my seat staring at her until Caroline poked me in the back.

I wasn't sure if I wanted to read my poem in front of everyone, but I stood up and took my paper from Mrs. Wakefield. It shook a little in my hands. I cleared my throat.

Hiding
The real me is hiding.

I thought that you were my disguise.
I thought that you blocked people's eyes.

Now you are gone, but I'm the same,
On my own, trapped in a game.

I do not like the me I see.
I wish that you were still with me.

Why did the real me go to hide?
Can I find her still inside?

The real me is hiding.

"Great job, Elise," said Mrs. Wakefield.

"I don't get it," said a boy named Greg.

"Elise, why don't you tell us a little bit about your poem?"

I thought. "I guess it's about things being different than they seem. And about . . . losing track."

"I think this poem is very interesting because it includes so many elements," Mrs. Wakefield said. "There's loss, self-reflection. Those are just a couple of them. Great work, Elise."

I sat down and glanced at Franklin. He didn't look up from the rocket ship he was designing on his gridded notebook page. I wondered if he'd even listened.

I read Mrs. Wakefield's comment on the paper: *I hope you share more of your great thoughts with me!*

Caroline beamed at me. Then she flicked a small piece of paper from the top of her desk to mine. I opened it.

It said,

See?

I smiled back.

• • •

Uncle Hugh and Aunt Bessie were happy when I showed them what Mrs. Wakefield had written. And that night it was easier to sit down and do my homework. I kept my math paper smooth and nice, and did all my graphing in sharp colored pencil. When I got it back two days later, there was a big check plus on it.

And when we had to recite a poem for Mrs. Wakefield, I practiced and practiced and remembered every single word.

Then a *really* good thing happened and that was that I studied enough for the next science test to get a ninety-five.

After that, my work didn't scare me anymore. I just did it, and things started to go well more often.

And then one day I came home to the library, and on my desk was the last key.

This room was probably the strangest of all, besides the room that had had nothing in it, of course.

There were no books or pictures, no journals or scrapbooks. There *was* a message. It said QUESTION.

A million pieces of paper with what looked like single sentences written on them were taped all over the walls.

I looked closer. They were all questions.

Some questions had quotations and a name underneath, and some were on their own, as if anyone could have asked them.

"Where did I leave my keys?"   —John

"Where are Elise's shoes?"   —Hugh

"How are you feeling today?"   —Bessie

"Please ice cream for dinner?"   —Elise

"Did anyone see where I put my book?"
                                    —Hugh

"Did you eat your vegetables?"   —Bessie

What is the point of this life?
Why do we have to grow up?
Does it matter that cheese is actually just really old milk?
"Why don't we ever have any beans when I need them?"
                                    —Hugh

"What is Hugh talking about?"   —John

"Do   elephants   think   really   big thoughts?"
                                    —Alec

"Well,   do   giraffes   think   really   tall thoughts?"
                                    —Jake

Why is the right thing to do so often the hardest thing to do?
"Can I color now?"   —Elise

There were too many to read all at once. And they made me a little sad, thinking of all those family moments I had forgotten.

But mostly I felt confused. I had opened every locked

room. I thought all my questions would be answered, but instead I'd found a million more.

"Elise, come to my desk, please."

Oh, super-great. I hadn't been in trouble at school in a long time.

But when I got to Mrs. Wakefield's desk, she handed me a note and said, "Caroline is absent today; her mom called and asked that you bring her homework, if you can. Here's her address."

"I can," I said. Phew. That was not scary after all.

When I sat down, nosy Amanda peered at the note.

"I'll bring Caroline her homework," she said. "She's my friend."

Mrs. Wakefield overheard and said, "Caroline's mother wants Elise to do it. Please don't worry, Amanda; it doesn't concern you."

See, Amanda, I thought. *Caroline is done with you.*

I paid attention to all the assignments that day so I would be a good homework-bringer. I didn't know who Caroline's locker partner was, so I couldn't get her books. But maybe she had some of the right ones at home already anyway, or I could lend her mine.

After I called Aunt Bessie to ask for a ride home later, I walked to the address on the paper. It was on Main Street, the same as Leonard's store. I remembered Caroline saying it was over the deli.

I let myself in the lower door, which was open, walked up the stairs, and knocked.

Caroline's mom answered. Her soft-looking clothes made me think of Aunt Bessie. "Oh, hello. You must be Elise." She gave me a big smile.

"Yep. I have Caroline's stuff."

"That's right . . . she said specifically to ask for you. I don't know why she couldn't just call someone, but here you are. She didn't come out all day, except to make a tuna fish sandwich at lunch. Why you'd eat stinky tuna in your bedroom, I don't know, but it's her room."

Caroline's mom seemed like the opposite of Franklin's mom. If Franklin's mom didn't understand having a friend stop by when you were sick or eating tuna fish in your room, then it wouldn't happen.

She let me into the apartment. The living room, dining room, and kitchen were all open to each other. Caroline's sisters played on the living room floor. They were maybe two and four, wearing pajamas in the late afternoon. They looked like mini Carolines.

"Her room's the last one down the hall. She's still resting."

I went to the end of the hall and knocked on Caroline's door. "It's Elise."

"Oh, come in!"

I opened the door. Caroline was dancing around in a white sweatshirt and pajama pants. She hopped over and shut the door behind me.

"Here's your homework list." I felt confused. This Caroline didn't look sick or resting.

"Thank you." She set the list on her desk. Then she looked at me with an expectant face.

"Okay, well, feel better?"

"Elise," Caroline whispered. "I have a secret."

"What is it?"

"It's asleep on my pillow."

I looked over at her bed. There was a tiny gray-striped kitten, curled up.

"Oh, cute!"

"Shhh, shhh!" Caroline hissed. "Secret!"

"Oh, right," I whispered, suddenly understanding the mystery of tuna-in-bed. "Can I hold him?"

"Sure." Caroline scooped up the kitten and handed him to me. We both sat on the bed.

"He's sweet and sleepy," I said. "Where'd he come from?"

"I rescued him. Found him outside, just dumped by the road. There were other kittens with him, but . . ."

I guessed they didn't make it. The look on Caroline's face . . . "Where does he go to the bathroom?"

"I have a little box for him in the closet."

I let the kitten go and he stumbled over to Caroline's lap. "I wasn't really sick today. I just wanted to stay with him."

"Um . . . how long can you keep him secret?"

"That's the thing. Probably no time at all. I've got to get him out of here. No room for extras at our house. Says Dad, anyway." She looked at me. "You guys have space. You could have a kitten."

"Can't. Uncle Hugh's allergic."

"Oh." Her face fell.

"I do know someone . . . who has never had a cat but is completely obsessed with them. She'd probably take him. Or at least find him a good home."

"You sure?"

I nodded. "Positive."

When Franklin saw me standing in front of his locker, he rolled his eyes and put a scowl on. I handed him a note. "You don't have to talk to me. This is for Diana. Tell her to be there today, after school. You can come, too, if you want."

"You want to hang out with Diana?"

"No, just . . . you'll see. Just see if you can get her there . . . in front of the deli."

Franklin shrugged. "Sure, whatever."

After school, when Caroline's mom took her sisters to their swimming lessons, Caroline and I put the kitten in a box and brought it down to the sidewalk. I wrote *Diana* on the box.

"Bye, Tommy," Caroline whispered to the kitten. "I'll miss you."

"Maybe you can go and visit." She seemed sad, so I slipped my elbow through hers as we walked upstairs.

We knelt on her couch, watching out the window.

"There they are!"

It was Franklin who noticed the box, pointed to it. Diana seemed puzzled, but opened it. Then she looked surprised and excited, and lifted Tommy out. Franklin was peering up and down the street, probably for me. He didn't look up, though, so he didn't see me. I giggled. For the first time in ages I thought about Franklin and actually felt happy, like laughing. Even without me, Franklin was out there, being Franklin.

We watched them walk away.

"Are you friends with her?" Caroline asked. "Diana?"

"No, but Franklin is."

"Why would you give her a kitten, if she isn't your friend?"

"I don't know." I paused. "It just seemed like the right thing to do."

We both turned back into the room and sat for a minute, in our own thoughts.

"Hey, Caroline?"

"Yeah?"

"Will you come over to my house? Maybe tomorrow? I want to show you something."

Caroline came home with me the next day. We went up to the room of questions and she read the walls for a long time. Then we sat on the floor. "What was in the other rooms?"

"Well"—I counted on my fingers—"there was a room about Mom, a room about Dad, a room about Uncle Hugh, a room about me and Dad together, Dad's library, a room about believing, an empty room, and this."

Caroline thought for a few minutes. "I'll be right back."

She returned with several sheets of paper, a marker, and a roll of masking tape from the library desk. "If you can't beat 'em, join 'em."

"What?"

"I don't think we'll solve this. I think we're supposed to join in. That's what the message says to do. What do you want to ask?"

"I don't know."

"Fine, I'll start." She knelt and wrote: *Why did Elise get a room full of questions?* She taped the paper to the wall.

"Your turn." She handed me the marker.

"I don't know what to write."

"Start with something easy."

I thought and *still* didn't know what to write.

Caroline took back the marker. She wrote, *Why do we have boogers?* and taped it up.

I laughed. "Do you really want to know the answer?" (Franklin probably knew it.)

"No." She laughed, too. "But it's a good question. Oh! I have another." She wrote and didn't let me see, then she hung the paper: *What would you put in your pocket if people had pockets like kangaroos?*

"Aren't those pouches?"

Caroline taped up a fourth paper: *What's the difference between pockets and pouches?*

By this point we were both giggling again.

Caroline handed me the marker. "Go on."

I wrote, *Why is the sky blue?*

"Good one," Caroline said as I added my question to the wall. "Now things we actually want to know."

She wrote: *Why do I hate getting sand between my toes?*

I thought, then wrote, *Why do beets taste so gross?*

Caroline laughed, and then became serious. "Okay. Real ones now. About things that matter."

I wrote: *Why did I get an empty room?*

And: *Where did all the keys come from?*

Then: *Will Franklin forgive me?*

Caroline looked at that, crossed it out, and wrote, *How can I show Franklin that I still want to be friends?* She squeezed my hand for a second, then let go.

I walked around the room, reading old questions that I hadn't looked at yet.

Then I came to this one:

What will my Elise be?

"Would you watch Ava for an hour?" Annie found me on the porch, waving to Caroline as she left with her mom.

"I don't know how."

"Don't be silly. You play with her all the time. She's been fed and changed and just needs someone to be with her. I want to run to the store with Bessie and we'll be in and out quicker without her. I wouldn't ask you if I didn't know it would be okay. And just in case, my cell-phone number is on the kitchen counter."

"Okay," I said. She handed Ava to me. She'd grown since she'd come to live with us.

Maybe Annie could see that in me, too, and not just Ava. Maybe that was why Annie wouldn't have left me alone in the house with Ava three months ago, but it was okay now.

Aunt Bessie and Annie left.

"Hi, Ava," I said, imitating Annie's gentle Ava-voice. "How about we go ride in the swing?"

I carefully pushed her legs through the openings in her swing, sat her down, buckled her in. Then I set the pace of the swing and stepped back. Ava was smiling, so I guess it was a good idea.

"Why are you here, Ava?"

Ava burbled.

"Why are you here, in my house?"

"Ous."

"Anyway, now I think it's good you're here."

"Goo?" she asked.

"Yes, goo."

That night, I collected all my messages from Dad.

There were seven.

QUESTION.
BELIEVE.
CHOOSE TO LIVE, CHOOSE TO LOVE.
KNOW WHAT YOU COME FROM.
SEEK TO LEARN.
UNDERSTAND THOSE YOU LOVE.
TREASURE YOUR LIFE.

I spread them out in a circle around me on my bedroom floor. They all seemed to be about deciding what was important in your life.

But there had been eight keys, and only seven messages, so what was that empty room for?

I could only imagine.

And then I realized: that was the point.

I knew what the eighth room was for.

It was for *me* to decide.

It could be whatever I needed it to be, whatever I wanted it to be.

And the truth, I suddenly understood, was that so could I.

Part III

Settling Up with Friends and Foes

The next morning I got up really early for a cooking project. Then Uncle Hugh drove me to school. I waited by Franklin's locker with a thermos of milk-free hot cocoa and an envelope.

When the bus kids started streaming in, I looked for Franklin. He seemed kind of gloomy.

"It's for you." I held out the thermos. "And this," I added, handing him an envelope. "You don't have to read it now. When you want to."

He took the envelope and the thermos and put them on the top shelf of his locker. I started to leave, but then I turned back and asked, "Do you hate me?"

Franklin took a minute to answer. "If I hated you, I would have turned you in."

I didn't know what to say to that, so I said, "We have a puzzle to finish, you know. I can't do it by myself. Uncle Hugh had to move it for Thanksgiving, but we should finish it before Christmas so Aunt Bessie can use the table for dinner." Franklin didn't say anything. "Well, anyway, read the note, if you want to." Then I managed to walk away.

Inside the envelope was a list:

TEN REASONS FRANKLIN IS A GOOD FRIEND

1. He's always willing to help, even if he could get in trouble for it.
2. He'll always cover for you to keep <u>you</u> from getting in trouble.
3. He's trustworthy.
4. He's so smart. He uses his ideas to help you, and he wants you to know all the interesting things he knows.
5. He's fun to spend time with.
6. He doesn't get mad at you if you call him names (though he doesn't deserve to be called them). He knows that he is none of those yucky things.
7. He seems at home at my house.
8. He has always been there, since I was little.
9. Things aren't the same without him.
10. He is forgiving.

PS I'm really, really sorry. I'm going to try harder to be a good friend from now on.

Later, I thought I could see the shadow of a hot-chocolate mustache on Franklin's upper lip.

I was sitting on the porch in my winter coat, waiting, when Franklin came by. I'd been hoping he would.

"Hi."

"Hi."

He sat down next to me.

We don't hug, so I knocked a light fist against Franklin's shoulder. Then we sat there for a few minutes, watching our breath curl and disappear in the cold air.

"So . . . you good?"

"I guess so."

"With me?"

"I don't know."

Why should he be? I took a deep breath. "I have to tell you some hard stuff."

"Hard stuff?"

"Yeah, like what's been up with me lately."

"Oh . . . go ahead." Then Franklin waited, in his usual Franklin way, ready to listen.

"At the beginning of the year, I started to feel embarrassed about some of the things we did together. I didn't like getting made fun of at school. But even before school started, something felt different, even when we were by ourselves."

"I embarrassed you?" Franklin asked.

I nodded. "I thought that some of the teasing and stuff would go away if I wasn't so close to you. So I tried to show that I wasn't. I'm really sorry that I did that."

"How sorry?"

"Really, really sorry. More sorry than I've ever been, about anything. I want to be friends still, even if—and I know maybe I blew it—even if it won't be the same."

Franklin thought for a while. I picked up a stick and started tracing the cracks between the wood slats of the porch.

"I was really mad at you," Franklin said finally. "You went from being the person who was nicest to me to the person who was meanest. Why didn't you just tell me what was going on?"

"I didn't know that was what was going on. I had to figure it out."

"What about Caroline? Are you still going to be friends with her?"

"Yeah," I said. "I really like Caroline. And what about the people you've been hanging out with? Are you going to hang out with them still?"

"Probably."

"That's okay," I said. "I've been thinking, because of the things Dad left me . . . the rooms and the messages. We have plenty of room for people . . . in our lives, I mean. Especially the ones who make us be the people we want to be. Because I really missed you, but I also missed . . . who I used to be with you . . . before. Do you know what I mean?"

He nodded.

"Do you remember when we pretended we'd found a cure for cancer?"

"Yeah."

"Do you think we could really find one?"

"Maybe, if we tried hard enough."

"That's how my dad died."

"We'd need a time machine, too, then?"

I nodded.

Franklin did some more thinking. He said, "Can I have more cocoa now?"

"Sure."

"No milk," he reminded me.

"I know."

We went inside and Franklin picked out some cookies and candy canes while I made the cocoa. Then we worked on our puzzle. There was a lot left, but we worked until all the stars were in place.

In the morning I visited my own, faraway locker and then went back to meet Franklin at his.

Suddenly, Amanda was there. Amanda, who had left me alone for weeks. She was *furious*.

"Listen, Scab-Picker. What you did is not okay with me. You stole my best friend!"

I stared at her. I knew what she was up to: a big fight in public, with her as the victim, to make me look like the jerk.

"I didn't steal anything!" I shouted. "Caroline is *sick* of you. She's sick of you because you're mean and disgusting and horrible. I don't know why anyone would want to be friends with you. You don't even care about Caroline. You only care about having people to follow you around so that you look cool. But you are really a big-time loser, and I'm not going to let you make me feel bad anymore."

Amanda looked like she'd been punched. It was even more fun to say all that stuff to her than it would have been to punch her.

I waited for her to yell at me. But she didn't. She just walked away.

Maybe that wasn't the end of it, but even though my heart was racing, I wasn't scared of her anymore.

"Nice," Franklin said.

"Thanks, Franklin."

He spun the dial on his lock, and we headed to class.

Keeping the Keys

With Christmas and vacation coming, it was a very busy week.

On Monday, Caroline and I went Christmas shopping. She helped me pick out something great for Franklin, a model space shuttle for him to build.

On Tuesday, Franklin and I studied at Caroline's for our big math test. She got us each a pair of reindeer antlers that blinked red and green lights and played "We Wish You a Merry Christmas." Franklin kept taking his off to figure out how they worked. Caroline squeezed mine to start the song again whenever I got the right answer. I must have heard it a hundred times!

On Wednesday, we had our math test and then the school holiday concert at night; I told Uncle Hugh and Aunt Bessie not to come because it was going to sound horrible, particularly the solo by Diana the cat girl, but they came anyway. They always do. Diana's singing turned out to be not completely horrible.

On Thursday, Aunt Bessie and I baked five dozen cookies for me to give to my teachers.

On Friday, we went to Uncle Beau's for a holiday dinner. Jake and Alec taught me how to play their new game system.

The next morning, the first of Christmas vacation, I found Uncle Hugh and Aunt Bessie at the kitchen table having breakfast. There was tons of food, so I helped myself to scrambled eggs, bacon, and Danish. I sat down and poured a mug of coffee. I took a swig and spat it back into the cup. "Ew."

"Allow me," Aunt Bessie said, taking the mug and dumping it out in the sink. She then refilled it halfway with coffee and added milk and Ovaltine. "Mocha." She handed it back.

I tasted it. "Much, much better. Thanks."

Now that school was finally over, I planned to start working on the empty room.

"Uncle Hugh, can you take me to get a few things?" I asked.

"Well, this morning I'm heading out to get our Christmas tree—does that interest you?"

"Yes!" It's very important that I help pick out our Christmas tree, because Uncle Hugh likes his trees short and fat and Aunt Bessie likes hers tall and skinny. I find the most in-between tree I can: medium height, medium plumpness.

Because it was vacation, I stayed in my pajama pants and just threw my vest on over my sweatshirt.

"More than anything else, a tree is what makes it feel like Christmas inside the house. Especially for your Aunt Bessie," Uncle Hugh said fondly in the car.

After about half an hour or so of wandering the rows of trees and debating, we had a happy tree strapped to the roof of our car. While Uncle Hugh and one of the boys at the tree lot were getting it ready, Uncle Hugh let me go to the little red and green stand where you pay, and look at the ornaments for sale. I bought a snowsuited baby in a sleigh that said BABY'S FIRST CHRISTMAS for Ava.

It took me, Uncle Hugh, and Leonard to get the tree in the house. Then we had to set it up straight in the stand, but Annie kept saying it was tipping to the right, and then we'd lean it the other way and Aunt Bessie would say it was tipping *left*. Finally, when the tree was up, I helped Aunt Bessie find the decorations in the attic.

Then I gave Annie Ava's little present.

"How wonderful!" she said. "This is Ava's first ornament. That was really thoughtful of you, Elise."

"I thought it might be nice, because it's also her first time coming to the family decorating. I thought something should be hers."

Then we tested all the strings of lights and fixed the broken ones.

The day was so busy that I didn't get a chance to think about working in the empty room. But that, I guess, was part of the point.

On Sunday morning, Aunt Bessie decorated the rest of the house. I helped her set out candles and put garlands on the mantels and banisters. Then she started on the next round of Christmas baking. I helped her roll out the dough and used the cookie cutters to press out stars, hearts, Christmas trees, angels, wreaths, bells, and snowmen. I mixed colored icing to decorate them with. Somehow I got covered with flour and confectioner's sugar.

The doorbell rang in the early afternoon.

Franklin!

"Hey! Merry Christmas!"

"Merry Christmas!"

"You're just in time to decorate cookies."

"Awesome."

I got Franklin an extra apron, and I made a big streak of flour across the front of it for him.

"Now it's like you've been here the whole time."

"Thanks."

And we set to work.

It was my first Christmas morning with someone younger around. Ava made it fun because there were a lot of Santa Claus presents for her and soon there was crumpled wrapping paper thrown everywhere and lots of noisy baby toys to catch her attention. She had recently learned to scoot around on her bum, but Annie was careful not to let her scoot too far in all the debris. Annie held her fingers so that she could stand up and not go anywhere while I showed her all her new toys.

Christmas dinner was in the dining room. Dresses for all the girls, even Ava, and suits for Uncle Hugh and Leonard. Annie held Ava in her lap, but she got passed around from person to person so everyone could eat. I took a turn with her during dessert. They said I could let her taste the cake and ice cream, so I fed her a little. She seemed to think cake and ice cream were the best foods ever, because she kept opening her mouth again and looking at me, and then she gave up waiting for me and stuck her hand right into my ice cream.

"Can I ask some questions?" I asked during a lull in the conversation. "Did Dad build those little rooms? When he was sick?"

Uncle Hugh and Leonard looked at each other.

"Don't forget that his brother's a carpenter and his best friend owns a hardware store," Aunt Bessie said. "Let's assume he had help. And there's the elevator to move stuff upstairs."

"So you were all in on it, from the beginning?"

"More or less," Leonard said.

"What do you think of it all, Elise?" Uncle Hugh asked. It made me feel grown-up, him calling me Elise and not Cricket.

"I think it was a good idea. I wouldn't have thought about things the way I do now without it. Like all those books would have been just something in the house that I didn't pay attention to, but now they mean something to me. And Miles the bear. You said I didn't like Miles when I was little, and he was about to fall apart back then, so it was nice that he was set aside because now he matters to me. And even the pictures. We have loads of pictures in the house, but I don't really look at them."

I paused for a minute, not sure if I was ready to talk about my secret hope.

"Part of me . . . wanted to think . . . that Dad was leaving the keys, that he was still here. But that wouldn't have made sense. He wouldn't have been hiding all that time. You had the keys, didn't you?" I asked Aunt Bessie.

"Two of them."

"And I had two," Uncle Hugh added.

And Leonard: "Me too."

"Whose was from California?"

"That was one of mine. Sent to a friend to send to you to keep you wondering," Leonard confessed.

"And two of them," I realized, "were from Dad himself. One left in the barn and one on the shelf in the library. But then why didn't you just give them to me? Why did you make me wait for years and years?"

"He told me—I don't know about anybody else—to wait until I thought you were ready," Uncle Hugh said. "You started opening the doors yourself, and, to be honest, I wasn't sure that you were ready. It was Bessie who gave you that next key. She said you must have learned what your dad hoped you would from the first room when you went to visit your mom."

"Why do you think he spread them out?" I asked.

"Well, each of us might have had different ideas of when you were 'ready,'" said Aunt Bessie.

"Are you all finished, then?" asked Leonard. "Have you gotten all the keys?"

"Yes, but I still have something left to do."

"What's that?"

"Take care of the empty room."

∙ ∙ ∙

When Christmas was over, it was finally time to focus on my project, and I had the whole rest of break to work on it. I asked Uncle Hugh if he could drive me to a few places and help me pay for a couple things. He took me to a drugstore to have several photos blown up, and then to a craft store to pick out frames and other supplies. Uncle Hugh paid for everything, without even saying anything about what it cost.

I took everything up to the empty room.

It wasn't so empty now.

On the last day of vacation, my friends came over.

Caroline got dropped off first.

"Hi, Elise!" She ran up the steps of the front porch, where I was waiting in my coat and gloves and scarf.

"Happy New Year!"

Soon Franklin arrived.

"Hi, Elise; hi, Caroline."

"I have something I want to show you guys," I said. "Come on."

I led them up to the no-longer-empty room.

On the walls were the pictures Uncle Hugh had helped me blow up and frame. One of him and Aunt Bessie. One of me playing with Ava at Christmas. One of Mom and Dad, and one of me and Dad. Several of me and Franklin growing up—

grinning without our front teeth, playing outside the summer we were seven, building a snowman when we were eight—and one of me and Caroline that Aunt Bessie had taken at the school holiday concert.

"Maybe we can get some more pictures," I said to Caroline.

"We will!"

On the opposite wall I'd taped artwork and school projects; my poem with Mrs. Wakefield's comment; my terrific science test.

I'd found a small table that Uncle Hugh said he didn't need anymore, so I brought that up in the elevator (finally! I got to ride in that elevator!). On the table, I put a composition notebook collaged with magazine cutouts of food called *Elise's Recipes* (inside were cooking instructions for things I'd helped Aunt Bessie make) and my sword from Knights.

Hanging above the table was a large key ring with seven keys. The eighth key was still on the chain around my neck.

"How did you know this was what you were supposed to do?" Franklin asked.

"I think Dad was saying, 'You can make this room whatever you want. You can make *you* whatever you want,'" I explained. "So I picked things that were most important to me."

"We'd like to be invited in, too," said Uncle Hugh from the doorway.

"Come in!" I said.

They took a look around. Aunt Bessie folded me into a hug. I could smell something to do with cooking on her clothes, and underneath that, her lavender soap. Her long braid brushed my cheek.

"Bess," Uncle Hugh said. "Come see this."

He had found the plastic paper-stand on the table.

It said:

TEN REASONS I AM GLAD TO BE ELISE BERTRAND

1. I have the Best Family in the Whole World (especially Uncle Hugh and Aunt Bessie).
2. I also have the Greatest Friends (Franklin and Caroline).
3. I'm learning to be a better friend.
4. I have all these great thoughts whirring in my head.
5. I'm doing better at school.
6. One day I'm going to be a great cook, like Aunt Bessie.
7. My mother loved me before I was even born.
8. My dad knew me for only a little while, but I know that he loved me because he took the time to make this puzzle for me, even though he was very sick.
9. I'm not going to let either of them down.
10. I'm not going to let myself down.

It was starting to get dark out.

"We ought to head in for dinner," Uncle Hugh said, and led Caroline and Franklin down the stairs.

Aunt Bessie turned back and called, "Sloppy joes. Don't miss them."

I looked at the room I'd filled. I felt so different than I had at my birthday.

"It's nice," I said, "for certain things to stay the same."

"Yes, it is," Aunt Bessie said. "Come on, my wonderful Elise."

I left the door open when I went downstairs.

About the Author

When Suzanne LaFleur was growing up, she loved spending time outside, swimming, reading, and writing. These are still her favorite things to do. She divides her time between Natick, Massachusetts, and New York City. Visit her on the Web at suzannelafleur.com.